Enid Blyton®
ANIMAL
STORIES

D0193269

Look out for all of these enchanting story collections

by Enid Blyton®

SEASONAL COLLECTIONS

Springtime Stories
Summer Holiday Stories
Christmas Tales
Christmas Treats
Winter Stories
Animal Stories
Summer Adventure Stories

OTHER COLLECTIONS

Brer Rabbit
Cherry Tree Farm
Fireworks in Fairyland
Mr Galliano's Circus
Stories of Magic and Mischief
Stories of Wizards and Witches
The Wizard's Umbrella

Enid Blyton®
ANIMAL
STORIES

h
Hodder
Children's
Books

HODDER CHILDREN'S BOOKS

This collection first published in Great Britain in 2019
by Hodder & Stoughton

1 3 5 7 9 10 8 6 4 2

A CIP catalogue record for this book is available from the British Library.

ISBN 978 1 444 94025 1

Printed and bound in Great Britain by Clays Ltd, Elcograf S.p.A.

The paper and board used in this book are made from
wood from responsible sources.

Hodder Children's Books
An imprint of Hachette Children's Group
Part of Hodder & Stoughton
Carmelite House
50 Victoria Embankment
London EC4Y 0DZ

An Hachette UK Company
www.hachette.co.uk
www.hachettechildrens.co.uk

Contents

The Kitten That Disappeared

The Kitten That Disappeared

JOHN AND ROSIE had a kitten of their own. It was three months old, as black as coal, with eyes as green as a cucumber. It was the merriest, lovingest, warmest little kitten you can imagine, and the two children loved it with all their hearts.

It was called Fluffy, and it always came when it heard its name. It was very mischievous, and loved to hide under the beds or under the chairs and pounce out at people's toes. Fluffy loved everyone and everyone loved Fluffy.

And then one day she disappeared. It was the most extraordinary thing. One minute she was playing with the two children in the kitchen and the next minute she was gone!

Mother was busy. It was Monday morning and she had a lot to do. She had washed up. She had done the laundry and put the dirty sheets and towels into the big basket for the laundry man to collect. She had made the beds and peeled some potatoes for dinner. And all the time Fluffy had played about with the children, sometimes jumping up at Mother, sometimes trying to catch her apron strings as she whisked here and there.

Then she was gone!

'Mother, where is Fluffy?' said Rosie, looking around.

'Hiding somewhere, I expect,' said Mother, fastening up the laundry basket in a hurry because she heard the laundry man coming down the passage.

'Fluffy, Fluffy!' called John – and there came an answering mew from somewhere, very tiny. 'MiiaOOOW!'

'She's somewhere!' said John, and the children began to look under the dresser and under the stove. The laundry man rang the bell, and Mother gave him the laundry basket. She shut the door so that Fluffy shouldn't run out if she were hiding somewhere. John called again. 'Fluffy! Fluffy!'

But no matter how he listened he couldn't hear another mew. No, Fluffy didn't answer at all. Rosie hunted under the bottom shelf of the broom cupboard, and then in the cupboard where the newspapers were kept. But Fluffy wasn't anywhere to be found!

'Oh, Mother, Fluffy has quite, quite disappeared!' said Rosie, almost crying.

'Don't be silly, darling,' said Mother. 'She must be somewhere about. She is hiding. Perhaps she has slipped upstairs and gone under one of the beds.'

'But, Mother, the kitchen door has been shut all the time,' said John. 'She simply must be in the kitchen if she is anywhere.'

'Well, she'll turn up all right,' said Mother. 'Don't

worry. I haven't time to help you hunt now, but when I've finished making this pudding for your dinner I will have a look around. But I expect by that time that Fluffy will come dancing out from somewhere!'

But, do you know, she didn't! So when Mother had finished making the pudding and popped it into the oven to cook, she had a look around for Fluffy too. She put down the saucer of milk and fish for the kitten, and called her.

'Fluffy, Fluffy, Fluffy! Puss, puss, puss! Dinner, dinner, dinner!'

But still no Fluffy came dancing out on black velvety paws! Rosie cried big tears.

'Mother, it's magic! Some fairy has taken Fluffy away!'

'Nonsense, darling!' said Mother, laughing. 'The fairies never do unkind things. Fluffy may be in the garden.'

So they put on their coats and hunted all around the garden. No Fluffy. They went to the house next

door, but Mrs Brown hadn't seen their kitten at all. They went to Mrs White's too – but she hadn't seen Fluffy since the day before.

Well, the children hunted and called all morning, but Fluffy was not found. They had their dinner, and then hunted again.

'Never mind,' said Mother. 'Fluffy will come in when she is hungry.'

'Mother, I don't think she ever went out,' said John. 'I don't really. One minute she was playing hide-and-seek with us, and the kitchen door was shut, I know – and the next minute she had disappeared.'

Although Mother put a saucer of fish and milk in the garden as well as in the kitchen, no Fluffy came to eat it – and Mother began to get worried too. She was very fond of the little black kitten and she could *not* think where it had got to. But at last she knew!

There came a ring at the kitchen door. Mother went to open it – and there was the laundry man, grinning all over his red cheerful face. In his hand he held a box.

'Good afternoon, Mrs Jones,' he said. 'I just wanted to tell you that you had sent this to the laundry, but as it seems quite clean we wondered if you really *did* want it washed!'

He opened up the little box he carried – and in it, curled up, was Fluffy! How the children shouted and danced for joy! Mother stared at Fluffy in astonishment.

'Whatever do you mean?' she asked the man.

'Well, madam, when we opened your laundry basket at the laundry, we found this little black kitten fast asleep inside!'

'Good gracious!' said Mother. 'She must have jumped inside when she was playing hide-and-seek with the children – and I didn't notice her – and shut down the lid! Then you took the basket away with Fluffy inside! We did hear a faint mew from somewhere – she must have been in the basket then!'

How glad Fluffy was to see the children again! How she pranced and danced on her four paddy-paws!

How she licked up her fish and milk! How she mewed and purred! What a fuss was made of her!

'Oh, Mother! Fancy sending our kitten to the laundry!' said Rosie. 'Suppose she had been washed and ironed, whatever would she have thought!'

It's a good thing the laundry *didn't* wash and iron Fluffy, isn't it? She *did* have a narrow escape!

The Tale of the Goldfish

The Tale of the Goldfish

ONCE UPON a time, thousands of years ago, there lived in China a merchant who was very fond of fishes. He kept four big ponds, and in each swam a different kind of fish, some little, some big, some brightly coloured and some speckled with silver spots. The merchant loved his fish and fed them every day.

He liked his bright-coloured fish the best. There were some that had blue streaks down their sides, and others that seemed to have caught a rainbow in their tails. The merchant leant over his ponds to watch his fish and longed for one thing – to breed a fish that was bright gold from nose to tail!

'There are plenty of silver fish,' he said to himself. 'There are many rainbow-coloured fish, and others that are spotted and speckled with brilliance. But no one in the whole world has ever had a fish that was all gold. How lovely it would be! How everyone would marvel! There could never be a prettier fish than a gold one, and it would give pleasure to all people, no matter where they lived.'

So he tried very hard to rear a fish that was all gold. But he found it was impossible. Some fish had bright yellow spots on them. Some had orange-coloured streaks. But none was all gold from tip to tail.

The merchant fell on bad times. He lost a great deal of his money, and became poor and shabby. He shut up his large house and lived in a small corner of it, without servants to wait on him. But he did not forget to feed his fish. He became an old man, and gave up the idea of rearing a fish of gold. He found that he was happy even though he was poor, and when his little grandchildren came to see him and climbed on his knees to listen to his stories he wished for nothing better.

One night a strange traveller came to the old merchant's house. The great bell outside the gate jangled to and fro as it had not done for years, and the merchant heard it in surprise. Who could be coming to his house now? He had no rich friends; they had all forsaken him.

He went through the long passages that led to the front gate and unbarred it. Outside stood a cloaked man, his horse beside him.

'Does Wong Fu, the great merchant, live here?' asked the visitor in a deep voice.

'Honourable sir, it is Wong Fu you see before you,' said the merchant, bowing, 'but I am no longer great. I am a poor man, and my house is empty. Enter, I pray you, for I will find you shelter and food, though it will not be of grand quality.'

The visitor stepped inside. The merchant took him

to a great marble basin where he might wash, and then slipped out to see to the horse. He stabled it in the empty stable, gave it food to eat and then went to prepare a meal for his unexpected guest.

In an old chest he had a few dainties stored away, and these he took out. Soon he had a meal ready and went to call his visitor. He found him leaning over the ponds, looking at the fish in the moonlight.

'You are fond of your fish, I see,' said the visitor, raising his head. 'They come swimming up to my hand, tame and friendly.'

'Yes,' said the merchant. 'It has always been the dream of my life to breed a fish all gold from head to tail – but I have never done so. Come, honourable sir, your supper is prepared.'

They sat down to eat, and at last the visitor told the old merchant who he was and why he had come.

'I am Sing Fu,' he said, 'the son of the old washerwoman you had many years ago.'

'But you are a wealthy man, well favoured and

wise,' said the old merchant in astonishment.

'It is so,' said the visitor. 'My mother put me in the service of Lai Tu the famous magician, and I found favour in his sight so that he made me like a son to him. Now Lai Tu is dead, and I have his wealth and much of his learning.'

The merchant got up and bowed himself to the ground, until his forehead touched the floor. He was in great awe of enchanters, and he trembled to think that he had one in his shabby house.

'Rise,' said the visitor. 'Do not kneel to me. My mother would not have you do that.'

'And is your honourable mother still alive and well?' asked the merchant, seating himself again, but still trembling in his surprise and excitement.

'She is well and happy,' said the enchanter gravely. 'It is by her request that I have come to see you. Do you remember her, honourable host?'

'Yes,' said the merchant at once. 'She was fat and jolly. She washed my linen better than anyone else.'

'And do you remember when she fell ill and could not work for five weeks?' asked the visitor.

The merchant felt uncomfortable. Had he treated the old washerwoman kindly? He could not remember. It would be dreadful if she had sent her son to punish him for an unkindness done to her years ago.

'No, I do not remember her illness,' he said at last.

'My mother remembers,' said the magician. 'You picked her up and carried her up to bed. You sent a doctor to make her well again, and you paid her wages all the weeks that she could not work. She has never forgotten. And now that she has a son who is wealthy and powerful she has asked me to go to all those who were once kind to her and reward them. So I have come to you.'

The old merchant was amazed.

'And do you also visit those who treated your mother ill?' he asked. 'Do you punish as well as reward?'

'No, for such is not my mother's wish,' said the enchanter gravely. 'She has forgotten her enemies, but not her welldoers. Now, honourable friend, you are poor and shabby. I bring you riches and honour, and they will bring you happiness.'

'There you are wrong,' said the merchant quietly. 'Neither riches nor honour bring happiness. I am happy now without them. I do not want gold, nor do I want servants, rich food, embroidered clothes. I am old and tired, but I am happy. Leave me as I am.'

The magician looked at the old man in wonder. Never before had he met anyone who refused what he had to offer. He said nothing more, and, bidding the merchant goodnight, lay down on a mat to sleep.

But in the middle of the night he went to his horse and took a sack from its back. In this sack were great bars of gold, which he had brought as a present for the old man. Now they would not be wanted. But the magician had thought of something splendid to do with them.

He took them to one of the ponds, where pretty grey-green fish were swimming, and one by one he slid the bars of gold into the water, murmuring magic words as he did so. Each bar dissolved into a cloud of orange-gold, and, behold, the fishes were attracted by the strange mist in the water and swam up in shoals to see what it was.

And when morning came each fish was bright orange-gold from head to tail! The old merchant saw them when searching for his midnight visitor, who had strangely disappeared. He stood by the pond, amazed and delighted. His dream had come true at last! Here were goldfish – bright gold from nose to tail!

And when you see a gleaming goldfish remember the kind-hearted merchant and his old washerwoman, and be kind to others yourself. You never know what magic you may start!

Good Dog, Tinker!

Good Dog, Tinker!

TINKER BELONGED to Robin and Mary. Sometimes he could be very good but at other times he could be very naughty. It didn't seem to matter which he was, though; the children loved him just the same.

One day Robin gave Tinker a juicy bone to gnaw. 'It's good for your teeth,' he said. 'And you've been such a good dog lately I think you really do deserve a bone!'

'Miaow!' said Tabby the cat. She liked bones too, though she could only scrape them with her rough tongue – she couldn't manage to chew them.

Tinker looked at her, with the bone in his mouth.

He dropped it for a moment and spoke to her.

'You can miaow all day if you like,' he said. 'But you won't get so much as one single sniff at this bone.'

'Wherever you bury it I shall find it,' said Tabby. She was very clever at finding where Tinker buried his bones, and he didn't like it. It was too bad to bury a half-chewed bone, and then, when next he came to dig it up, to find that it wasn't there because Tabby had found it.

'I shan't bury it this time,' said Tinker. 'I shall hide it where you will never be able to find it!'

He trotted off with the bone. He took it into the dark tool shed, and lay down to chew it. It was a very hard bone and Tinker couldn't crunch it up. He had a lovely half-hour of chewing and gnawing. Then he heard Robin whistling for him.

'Walkie, walkie, Tinker!' called Robin, and Tinker knew he must put away his bone and go. But where should he put it? It must be somewhere clever, where Tabby would never find it. Tinker thought of all the garden beds in turn. No, Tabby would hunt in each one. Then he looked around the tool shed. Tabby never came in here! He would hide his bone somewhere in the tool shed.

He was lying on a sack. What about tucking it inside the sack? Then no one would see, and it would wait here for him to come back and chew it. That would be a fine hiding place.

So Tinker pushed his lovely smelly bone into the sack, and then scampered off to join Robin and Mary.

He forgot about his bone till the evening. Then he wanted it again. Off he went to the tool shed to have a good chew. But, alas for poor Tinker, the door was shut fast! He stood and whined at it; he scraped it with his paw. But it was no use – the door wouldn't open.

'Bad luck, Tinker!' said Tabby nearby. 'I suppose you've got your bone hidden in there! And you can't get at it. Dear, dear, what a pity to hide a bone in a silly place like that.'

'Well, if I can't get it, you can't either,' said Tinker with a growl, and ran off.

The next day nobody went to open the tool shed to get out the tools. Poor old Tinker ran to the shed a dozen times that day, but he couldn't get in, and he couldn't manage to make Robin and Mary understand that he wanted to have the door opened.

So he had to go without his bone. Tabby sat and laughed at him, and when he ran at her in a rage she jumped up on to the bookcase and sat and laughed at him there. She really was a most annoying cat.

Now, that night somebody went to the tool shed. It was midnight and everyone in the house was fast asleep. The somebody was a robber. He had come to steal as many tools as he could out of the shed!

He was very quiet, so no one heard him, not even Tinker. He crept to the shed and found it locked. But he guessed that the key was not very far away, and he soon found it hung on a nail just under the roof of the shed.

He opened the door and slipped inside. He switched on his torch and looked around at the tools. They were very good ones, and kept beautifully. The man grinned. Just what he wanted! He would be able to sell them for a lot of money. He took them down quickly from their nails and put them quietly together.

I'd better slip them into a sack, in case anyone sees me on my way home, thought the robber. *I might meet the village policeman on his rounds*. He looked about for a sack and saw one on the ground. It was the one that Tinker had pushed his bone into. The bone was still there, very, very smelly now. The robber picked up the sack and shook it. The bone slid to the bottom and stayed there.

The man quietly put all the tools into the sack, and then put the bundle over his shoulder. It was terribly heavy. The robber went out of the door, locked it, and hung up the key again.

He went softly to the bottom of the garden. He

put down the sack and squeezed through the hedge, pulling the sack after him.

Then he put it on his shoulder again. He walked across the field with it, but it felt so heavy that he had to put it down on the ground again.

'I believe I could drag this sack across the field more easily than I could carry it,' said the robber to himself. 'It won't matter at all if it makes a bit of a noise now, because I am well away from any of the houses.'

So he dragged the sack over the field. He came to another hedge and squeezed through it. He went down a lane, still dragging the sack, and then, when he heard footsteps, he crouched down behind a bush, listening.

It was the village policeman. He had not seen or heard the thief, and he went slowly down the lane, thinking of the hot jug of cocoa that would be waiting for him when he got home.

The man crept out from his hiding place and carried on down the lane. He came to the wood and slipped in among the dark trees. He made his way through the wood until he came to a big bank where he knew there were a lot of rabbit holes. He pushed the sack down a very big hole and pulled bracken and bramble sprays over the entrance.

I'll come and get the tools when everyone has forgotten about them, he thought. Then off he went home.

Now, in the morning, Tinker ran to the tool shed early, for he knew the gardener would be there at eight o'clock to open the door. Sure enough, the man soon came along whistling. He took down the key and opened the door. Tinker darted in.

But the sack was gone! Tinker gave a howl of dismay – and at the same time the gardener gave a shout of surprise.

'Hey! What's happened to all the tools? They're gone!'

Tools! Who cares about tools! thought Tinker. *It's my bone that is really important. Oh, tails and whiskers, wherever can it be?*

The gardener went off to tell the children's father, and Tinker flew off to ask Tabby if she knew anything about his bone.

There was a great disturbance about the lost tools. The policeman was told and he came hurrying up to the house.

Nobody paid any attention at all to poor Tinker and his lost bone. Tabby laughed at him.

'You needn't laugh!' said Tinker. 'It was an important bone, and the robber stole that as well as the tools. I do wish I knew where it was.'

'Well, go and sniff about and see,' said Tabby, beginning to wash herself.

Tinker thought that was a good idea. He ran to the tool shed. Yes, he could smell exactly where his bone had been hidden in the sack in the corner. He ran out of the shed and began to sniff around the garden, hoping to get a smell of the bone somewhere.

When he came to the hedge at the bottom he got very excited. There was the smell of bone there quite distinctly. That was where the robber had put down the sack to squeeze through the hedge. The sack smelt strongly of bone and the smell had been left on the ground beneath the hedge. Tinker had a very sharp nose and he could easily smell it.

He squeezed through the hedge. He ran into the field and sniffed about. He could smell nothing – till suddenly he came to the spot where the burglar had put his sack down and had begun to drag it instead. With his nose to the ground Tinker followed it across the field to the second hedge, through the hedge and out into the lane.

Fancy the robber taking my bone with him in the sack such a long way! thought Tinker. *It must have seemed a very fine and important bone to him. Now, here we go again – down the lane – behind this bush – down the lane again – and into the wood. Off we go – through the trees – to this bank – and, oh,* what *a strong smell of bone there is near this hole!*

Tinker scraped away at the rabbit hole, sniffing his bone all the time. It was in the sack of tools, pushed down the hole. Tinker couldn't get it out.

I'll go back and get Robin and Mary to help me, he thought. So he trotted back in excitement, and by pulling at Mary's skirt and Robin's trousers he managed to make them understand that he wanted them to follow him.

In great astonishment they went down the garden, through the hedge, across the field, through the second hedge, into the lane, and then into the wood to the big rabbit warren.

And there Tinker showed them the sack in the rabbit hole. 'My bone's in there,' he woofed to them. 'Get it out, please.'

But Robin and Mary were not at all interested in the bone – they shouted with joy to see the tools in the sack!

'Daddy's tools! Look, they're all here! Let's take them home this very minute. Won't Daddy be pleased? Oh, you very, very clever dog, Tinker, to find them for us!'

Tinker trotted home beside them, sniffing his bone eagerly. What a fuss there was when the children arrived home with all the tools!

They were emptied out and counted. Yes, they were all there! 'Tinker, you shall have a very big, extra-juicy bone today, for being so clever!' said Robin.

Well, that was good news. Robin rushed off to get the bone from the butcher's, and Tinker put his head inside the empty sack and dragged out his beautiful old bone as well!

'I must say you were terribly clever to find all of the things that were stolen by the robber,' said Tabby in a very admiring sort of tone. Tinker was extremely proud.

'Well, I am rather a clever dog, you see,' he said, 'and as you seem to have learnt that at last I'll show you that I'm a very generous dog too – you can have this bone, and I'll have the new one when it comes! And I say – have you heard? The policeman is going to hide in the wood till the robber comes to fetch the tools he hid. Then he'll be caught! I'm going to hide too. I shall have fun!'

Tinker did enjoy his bone – and Tabby enjoyed the other one too. Wasn't it a good thing Tinker hid his first bone in the sack?

Clever Old Budgie

Clever Old Budgie

EVERY EVENING after tea, Robert and Bessie opened their budgerigar's cage and let out the excited little bird.

'Come on, Budgie, dear little Budgie, spread your wings and fly!' said Robert. 'Come on to my head, if you like!'

'Talk, Budgie, talk!' said Bessie. 'Say 10345!'

'Don't be silly, Bessie!' said Robert. 'What's the sense of teaching our budgie a silly thing like our telephone number?'

'He might escape one day and then if he said our telephone number, somebody might guess what he was saying and telephone us,' said Bessie. 'It's *not* a silly idea. You're silly to teach him "Rockabye-Baby". Why don't you teach him a sensible song?'

'Well, he says "rockabye" so well,' said Robert. 'Soon he'll get the whole line – and the tune too! Budgie, listen: "Rockabye-Baby, on the treetop."'

'Rockabye, rockabye,' said the little green and blue budgie, his head on one side. '10345, rockabye 10345.'

'There – you've muddled him with your silly telephone number!' said Robert crossly. 'Please don't teach it to him any more.'

'He knows it now,' said Bessie. 'Ask for your dinner, Budgie! Say, "Where's my dinner?"'

'Where's my dinner?' said Budgie in his funny little voice. 'Dinner, 10345.'

He flew all about the room, sitting on the lampshade, then on the curtain pelmet, then on the top of the clock. Bessie held out her finger and he flew on to it at once, making a funny little noise in his throat.

The budgerigar was very sweet, and very tame. Robert and Bessie loved him, and Robert felt proud whenever the tiny bird flew on to his shoulder and pretended to whisper in his ear.

Budgie had a lovely cage with a little mirror, and a bell he could ring. Sometimes he rang it so often that Bessie said it sounded as if little Noddy was somewhere in the room, ringing the bell on his blue hat!

One day Joe came to tea, and he couldn't take his eyes off the budgie. Tinkle-tinkle-tinkle, went the little bell, and, as soon as Joe looked up to the cage, the budgie put his pretty head on one side and spoke clearly:

'Rockabye, dinner, dinner, dinner!'

'Isn't he marvellous?' said Joe. 'I do wish I had a bird like that! Will he come out of his cage? Is he tame?'

'Oh, yes – he always comes out after tea,' said Bessie. 'He may fly on your head, Joe, so don't be surprised!'

After the tea was cleared away, Mother left the children to amuse themselves. Joe wanted the budgie out of his cage, of course, and Bessie went to get him.

'Shut the window, Joe,' she said. 'It's open and we mustn't let Budgie fly away. He wouldn't know how to feed himself, and he might die.'

Joe slid the top part of the window upwards – but he didn't quite shut it. He didn't notice that there was a small space still left at the very top. He was so anxious to see the budgie come out of his cage. Out he came, and flew straight to Robert, sitting on his hand and pecking at his nails. 'Dinner, dinner,' he said, and Robert laughed.

'No, my nails aren't your dinner. Don't, Budgie!'

Joe spoke to the tiny bird. 'Say my name,' he said. 'Joe, Joe, Joe! Say Joe!'

'10345,' said the budgie, his head on one side.

'What's that he said?' asked Joe, surprised.

'It's a silly thing Bessie has taught him to say,' said Robert. 'Our telephone number! Budgie, say

"Rockabye-Baby on the treetop". Go on now – you said the whole of it yesterday!'

'No – say "Joe, JOE"!' said Joe in such a loud voice that Budgie was frightened. He flew off Robert's hand at once with a little squeak, and went to the pelmet of the curtain above the window. He stood there, peering down cautiously. Then he felt the little draught that came in through the open space at the top of the window, and flew down to see where it came from.

And in one moment he was gone! He hopped on to the top of the open window, slid through the little space there, spread his wings – and vanished!

Bessie screamed. 'Oh! Budgie's gone! Joe, you didn't shut the window properly – you left a crack at the top. Budgie's gone!'

They all raced out into the garden. 'Budgie, Budgie, Budgie, where are you? Budgie, come back!' they called.

But no Budgie was to be seen anywhere. Where

could he be? The children called him and hunted in the garden from top to bottom till it was dark.

'It's no good,' said Robert at last. 'He's gone. Goodness knows where! He won't last long because he can't feed himself properly – and a cat might get him. Blow you, Joe – leaving the window a crack open!'

Bessie was in tears. Mother comforted her and went to ring up the police station to report the loss. It was dreadful to think of the little budgie out in the darkness all by himself. He had never been out of doors before. What a big, frightening world it would seem to him.

'Will the other birds help him?' asked Bessie tearfully. 'Will they show him where to sleep at night? Will they tell him to beware of cats?'

'Perhaps,' said Mother. 'Now stop worrying about him. Maybe someone will telephone to the police station to say they have found him.'

But nobody telephoned the police that night nor the next morning. And then suddenly their own telephone rang, and a voice spoke clearly.

'Hello! Is that 10345?'

'Yes, it is,' said Robert, who was answering the telephone because his mother was busy. 'Can I take a message to my mother for you?'

'Well, I rang up to know if you had lost a beautiful little budgerigar,' said the voice.

'Oh, *yes* – we have!' said Robert. 'Is he all right?'

'Well, he's a bit scared,' said the voice. 'He's in my garden, and he won't let me catch him.'

'However did you know he might be ours?' said Robert.

'My little boy saw him first,' said the voice, 'and when he went out to see what kind of bird was sitting in our plum tree the bird spoke to him – he was so surprised – and it said 10345 over and over again. So my little boy came running in and said that the bird must be telling him its telephone number, and please would I telephone to see if a budgie lived at that address!'

'Oh – clever Budgie!' said Robert. 'It *is* our

telephone number. What's your address? We'll come and fetch him.'

'We live at Tall Chimneys, Scotts Lane,' said the voice. 'I'll tell my little boy to keep his eye on the budgie till you come. Fancy him knowing his own telephone number!'

Robert ran to tell Bessie and his mother.

'There! I was *very* sensible to make him learn his telephone number, wasn't I?' said Bessie, overjoyed. 'Oh quick – let's go and get him. Mummy, will you take us in the car?'

'Of course,' said Mother. 'Go and open the garage, Robert, while I get my coat. We must go at once, or Budgie might fly away from the garden he's in.'

They were soon at Tall Chimneys, where a small boy was waiting for them at the gate. 'Hello – you've been quick!' he said, opening the gate to let the car through into the little drive. 'Budgie's still here. I almost thought he was going to fly on to my hand once, but he didn't. Come on, he's over here!'

He led the two children down a little path to a summerhouse – and there, sitting on a creeper that climbed all over it, was Budgie!

'Budgie!' called Bessie, excited. 'Dear Budgie. We've come to take you home!'

Budgie gave a little squawk of joy and flew straight to Bessie's outstretched hand. She covered him gently with her other hand so that he could not fly away again.

Robert had brought a little travelling cage with him, and Budgie was soon safely inside, the door shut on him. '10345,' he called. '10345.'

'There – that's what he kept saying,' said the little boy. 'At first I didn't know what he was talking about, then suddenly I wondered if he could possibly be saying his telephone number.'

'He was! I taught him,' said Bessie, red with pride. 'But Robert thought it was a silly idea, didn't you, Rob?'

'Yes. But I don't now. I think it was a marvellous

idea of yours,' said Robert. He turned to the small boy. 'Thank you very much for phoning us. We're so glad to get our little budgie safely back!'

And off they went with him, laughing to hear him squawking crossly in his tiny travelling cage. How glad he was to see his own big cage again! He hopped inside, rang his bell loudly, and looked at himself in the mirror.

'Rockabye, dinner, dinner,' he said.

'It's a good thing you didn't say *that* to the little boy!' said Bessie. 'Clever old Budgie!'

'Clever old Bessie!' said Mother and Robert together. And I agree with them – clever old Bessie!

The Cow That Lost Her Moo

The Cow That Lost Her Moo

THERE WAS once a pretty cow called Buttercup. Everyone was very fond of her, for she was a gentle creature, though rather stupid. She lived in a big field with twelve other cows, and she was the prettiest of the lot.

One day she caught a cold and she lost her voice. She tried her hardest to moo loudly just as she had always done – but it wasn't any good at all. Not the tiniest bit of moo came out of her big mouth. Buttercup had no voice except a small whisper that sounded rather like dry leaves rustling together.

This will never do! thought Buttercup to herself in a

great fright. *I* must *get some sort of voice. I can't go about whispering. Even the ducks on the pond over there have a louder voice than I have. If I can't moo perhaps I can learn to quack!*

So that night, when the little folk came running out into the fields, Buttercup whispered to one of them.

'Pinkity, I've lost my lovely moo. Could you get me another one, do you think? Or at any rate could you get me another voice of some sort? I hate talking in a whisper like this; it is so stupid for a large cow like me to have such a tiny, whispery voice.'

Pinkity looked at the large cow and grinned all over his cheeky little face. 'I can't get you a moo,' he said. 'But I could get you a quack, if you like! I know those ducks would spare me one if I asked them.'

Buttercup nodded her head. Off went Pinkity, spoke to the ducks, and came back with something wrapped up in a dock leaf. 'Here you are,' he said to the grateful cow. 'Swallow this and you'll find you have a fine new voice!'

So Buttercup swallowed the dock leaf with the quack spell inside – and at once she found that she could quack!

You should have heard her! Really, it was funny to hear a big cow quacking away for all she was worth. Her friends came round her in surprise.

'Why do you quack?' they asked. 'You are very foolish, Buttercup. The farmer will think you are a duck, and will put you on the pond to swim with the others. You will have to lay eggs for him.'

'Quack, quack!' cried Buttercup in a great fright. 'I couldn't lay an egg! I know I couldn't! And I should die of fear if I had to swim on the pond! Pinkity, where are you? Quack, quack, quack! Take away this quack and bring me some other voice. I can't bear it!'

Pinkity hopped up. He was very much enjoying himself. He caught a loud quack as Buttercup spoke, and wrapped it up in another dock leaf. He put it into his pocket and hurried off. He went to a brown mouse for a little squeak. She gave it to him wrapped up in a daisy leaf, for it was very small.

He ran back to Buttercup and gave it to her. She swallowed it – and then began to squeak in a very high voice, just like the mouse. All the other cows began to moo with laughter.

'Buttercup, how foolish you are!' they said. 'Now you have a voice like a mouse. The weasel will come along when he hears you, and will try to bite you, thinking you are a mouse – and the big owl will swoop down on you.'

'Too-whoo-too-whoo!' called the owl in the distance. Buttercup began to tremble. She was in a great fright.

'Pinkity, Pinkity!' she squeaked. 'Come here! Take away this squeak, I beg of you, and bring me a better voice. I can't bear this. Squeak, squeak. Eeeeeeee!'

Pinkity took away the squeak and ran off again, beaming.

This was a great joke. What a tale to tell when he went home in the morning!

This time he went to a sheep lying down on the hillside, and asked her to lend him her baa. She did so, and he carried it off, wrapped up in two nettle leaves. Buttercup swallowed it gratefully and at once began to baa and bleat in a most sheep-like manner.

All her friends stared at her in amazement. Whatever would she do next?

'Buttercup, are you turning into a sheep?' asked Daisy, a pretty white cow.

'No,' said Buttercup. 'Of course not. I am a cow. Baa-aa! Baa-aa!'

'Well, the farmer will be sure to think you are a sheep if you baa like that,' said Daisy. 'He will expect you to grow wool for him and will clip your coat just as he does those of the sheep. My! You will be cold with all your coat clipped away!'

Buttercup was horrified. What? Have her nice hairy coat clipped away so that she might grow a thick covering of wool? Never! 'Baa, baa, baa!' she bleated to Pinkity. 'Oh, do take this voice away quickly. I can't bear it. Baa, baa!'

Pinkity hopped up and took it away. He gave it back to the surprised sheep, and then hunted around for someone else who might lend him a voice. He met Bobby, the dog, out rabbiting by himself in the moonlight, and he called to him.

'Hey, Bobby! Will you lend me your bark for a little while?'

'No,' said Bobby. 'I want it.'

'Now, listen, Bobby,' said Pinkity. 'I'll show you the best rabbit hole in the field if you'll lend me your bark for a time. Please do. I'm having such fun with a foolish cow. I've made her quack, squeak and baa. Now I want to make her bark.'

'Well, mine's a very *fierce* sort of bark,' said Bobby. 'She will frighten all the other cows if they hear it. So I warn you, Pinkity . . . you'd really better not borrow it!'

But Pinkity said yes, he really must have it. So Bobby gave it to him, wrapped up in a piece of paper he found in the ditch. Off went Pinkity over the fields to Buttercup. 'Here you are,' he said, giving her the bark in the piece of paper. She ate it up, paper and all.

And then, stars and moon! She began to bark like a very fierce dog!

'Wuff, wuff, wuff! Grrrrrrrr! Wuff, wuff, wuff, wuff! GRRRRRRRRRR!'

There had been a growl mixed up with the bark, and so Buttercup growled as well as barked. The other cows, who all disliked and feared dogs, were terrified almost out of their lives. They rushed off to the other end of the field in a fright.

As for Buttercup, she was terribly frightened too! She hated dogs, and this bark and growl she had made her very much afraid. She galloped away – and trod so heavily on Pinkity's toes that he yelled with pain. He limped off crying big tears down his cheeky little face, and went home to bathe his poor foot.

So when Buttercup went to find him to beg him to take her bark away he was nowhere to be seen! No, he was safely at home, tying up his poor squashed toes in a bandage, wishing very much that he hadn't played such silly tricks on foolish Buttercup!

Buttercup barked all through the night, and growled when she wasn't barking. Her friends were so frightened of her that they wouldn't let her come near them.

'If you come any nearer, we will run our horns into you!' they cried. 'You are turning into a dog, there's no doubt! You will have to live in a kennel and eat biscuits and bones, instead of sweet grass.'

Buttercup was very unhappy. She went away into a corner and barked all to herself. *Why did I bother about my voice?* she thought sadly. *I would rather have no moo at all than bark like a dog. This is dreadful. What will the farmer say when he milks me?*

The farmer was scared and puzzled when he heard Buttercup's new voice. He stared at her as if he couldn't believe his ears. A cow barking? What next?

'Wuff, wuff!' said Buttercup, hanging her head in shame. 'Wuff, grrrrr!'

'I shall have to sell you, Buttercup,' said the farmer, seeing how frightened of her all the other cows seemed to be. 'I can't have a barking cow.'

'Wuff, grrr!' said Buttercup most unhappily. She couldn't bear the thought of being sold. It would be dreadful to leave the fields she knew and go somewhere strange.

All that day she barked and growled, and when night came she looked out anxiously for Pinkity. That rascally little creature had been feeling sorry that he had played such tricks on Buttercup. His toes were very painful, and he thought it must be a punishment for him.

I'd better go out and see how Buttercup is tonight, he thought to himself. *Even though I can hardly walk, I must certainly go.*

So out he went into the field. No sooner had he gone

through the gate than he almost jumped out of his skin. He heard what seemed to him to be a very fierce dog barking and growling just above him. Of course, it was Buttercup waiting for him. What a fright he got!

'Wuff, wuff, grrrrr!' said Buttercup. 'Do pray take this terrible voice away, Pinkity. Wuff! I frightened everyone and myself too. I would rather have no voice at all. It was foolish of me to want one.'

Pinkity took the bark and growl away and wrapped them carefully in his handkerchief. Then he limped off to find Bobby, who, he was sure, would be wanting his bark badly.

So he was. He was very angry indeed about it!

'You said you only wanted my bark for a little while!' he scolded. 'Here I've had to be all day without either my bark or my growl and couldn't even bark at an old tramp who came and stole some eggs. So I got a beating for not doing my duty. Give me my bark at once!'

Pinkity gave it to him – and then forgot all about

his bad foot, for angry old Bobby chased him up the lane and over the fields, barking at the top of his voice!

'Wuff! You mischievous creature! Grrrr! You scamp, you rogue! Wuff, grrr, wuff!'

Buttercup was very thankful indeed to have lost her bark. She ate grass quietly, and when her friends saw that she no longer barked or growled they came round her once again and talked to her.

And suddenly she found herself mooing to them! Yes, her cold had gone away, and she had got her own voice back once more! It had gone only for a little while whilst she had a cold. So she needn't have worried herself so much after all!

'To think I had a quack, a squeak, a baa, a bark and a growl!' said Buttercup to herself in shame. 'When all the time, if only I'd been patient, my own voice was just waiting to come back. Really, I am a very foolish cow! I do hope the farmer won't sell me now.'

He didn't, of course. When he found that Buttercup was her own self again, and mooed just as she always did, he patted her and said, 'Well, well, I can't think what happened to you yesterday, Buttercup – but you seem all right today, so, as you give me a nice lot of creamy milk, I shan't sell you!'

'Moo, moo, moo!' said Buttercup, and whisked her tail happily. Then she whisked it again and knocked off the farmer's hat. But he didn't seem to mind!

A Little Bit of Magic

A Little Bit of Magic

FANNY HAD been reading a book of fairy tales. My goodness, the magic there was in Fairyland! The way wizards changed people into different things – and the way that spells were worked and magic done – it was wonderful!

'Oh, Mummy!' she said when she had finished the book. 'I wish I could see some magic. But I don't believe there is any nowadays. Things don't change suddenly into something else – there don't seem to be any spells about at all.'

'Well, I can show you something that seems like magic,' said her mother. 'Something that happens a hundred times every year, in everyone's garden.'

'Show me, Mummy!' said Fanny, really excited.

So her mother took her out into the garden. She went to the cabbage patch and hunted about. She turned back a leaf with holes in and showed Fanny a green and yellow caterpillar there.

'We'll take this caterpillar on a piece of leaf, and watch him use a spell to change himself into something else,' she said.

So she and Fanny took the little caterpillar to Fanny's bedroom on a piece of cabbage leaf. Mother found a box and made holes in it. She put a piece of glass over the top so that Fanny could watch the tiny creature eating his cabbage leaf.

'Has anyone told you what a caterpillar can turn himself into?' asked Fanny's mother. But Fanny was only six, and she didn't know.

'Well, this caterpillar can turn himself into a butterfly with wings,' said Mother.

'However can he do that?' said Fanny in surprise,

looking at the long caterpillar. 'I can't see the beginnings of any wings at all.'

'He hasn't got even the beginnings now,' said her mother. 'He gets those later when the magic begins to work. We will watch him each day.'

So they watched the caterpillar. Twice he grew so fat that he had to change his tight skin. Fanny was surprised to find he had a new one underneath each time. She gave the little caterpillar a new cabbage leaf every day and he grew and grew.

One day he didn't want to eat any more. He went to a corner of the box and began to spin a kind of silky web there. Fanny couldn't think where he got it from.

But he had plenty of silk. He fixed himself safely in the corner – and then a strange change came over him. He changed his skin for the last time. He lay still. He became hard and brown. He seemed quite, quite dead.

'He seems just a hard little case,' said Fanny, puzzled. 'He isn't like a caterpillar any more. But he isn't like a butterfly either. His magic must have gone wrong, Mummy.'

'We'll wait and see,' said Mother. 'We call him a chrysalis now. Watch carefully each day.'

Fanny watched – and one day she was very excited. 'Mummy, Mummy! I believe there is a butterfly being made inside the caterpillar's hard brown case! I can faintly see the outline of wings – and what looks like new legs all bunched up together! Look!'

Her mother looked – and as she looked, a magical thing happened. The case split down the back! It began to move and wriggle – and suddenly, out of the split, came a small head!

'Something's coming out – something's coming out! Look!' squealed Fanny.

Something did come out – something with four white crumpled wings, six thin legs, and a head with pretty, trembly feelers on it! Something so unlike a caterpillar that it was quite impossible to think there had ever been a caterpillar inside the case.

'It's a pretty white butterfly!' said Fanny. 'A butterfly with wings! Mummy, how did it grow wings? It hadn't any when it turned into a chrysalis. How can a caterpillar turn into a butterfly? Do, do tell me.'

'I don't know,' said her mother. 'Nobody knows. It's a little bit of magic. The caterpillar goes to sleep and wakes up as a butterfly. It's like the tale of *Beauty and the Beast* – you remember how the ugly Beast turned into the beautiful Prince? Well, that's the same sort of thing that the caterpillar does.'

'It's real magic,' said Fanny, watching the butterfly dry its crumpled wings in the sunshine. 'Soon it will fly away and be happy in the flowers. It won't eat cabbage-leaves any more. It's a butterfly!'

Have you watched this bit of magic? You ought to. It's just as strange as anything that happens in Fairyland, isn't it?

The Noah's Ark Lion

The Noah's Ark Lion

KATIE HAD a big Noah's ark. It was a lovely one, and besides the Noah family, there were two of every animal you could think of! Lions, tigers, bears, horses, goats, dogs, giraffes, elephants, ducks, turkeys, pigs – there didn't seem to be any animal that wasn't there!

Katie had a lovely time playing with them each day. She set them out in twos and made them walk into the ark with Mr and Mrs Noah. They liked this very much.

But at night the Noah's ark animals had even better fun! Mr Noah opened the door of the ark and let them all out to play! My goodness me, what fun they had then!

They all tumbled out on to the ground and played whatever game they liked best. The ducks and the hens played hide-and-seek, the giraffes and the elephants played touch-me-last, and the white and brown bears played kiss-in-the-ring. Mr and Mrs Noah, and Shem, Ham and Japheth, their wooden children, watched them and laughed.

When it was time for all the animals to go back into the ark they were lined up in twos and marched in quietly. Then Mr Noah shut the door after them and they all lay quietly in the ark without moving, waiting for the time to come when Katie would open the lid and take them out.

Now, all the animals were very good except the lion. He thought a great deal of himself ever since he had heard Katie call him the king of the beasts. He wandered off each night by himself, for he thought he was too grand to play games with the others. He sat by the fire and curled his long tail round him. Sometimes he nibbled a bit of the hearth rug. Sometimes he climbed up to the clock on the bookshelf and listened to its funny ticking voice.

And when he heard Mr Noah calling all the animals back into the ark the lion turned up his brown nose and stayed where he was! He didn't want to go into the ark. Wasn't he the king of all the beasts? Why should he be hustled into the ark like the stupid ducks and hens and pigs? Mr Noah got so cross with the lion.

'Where's that lion tonight?' he would say. 'He is just too tiresome for anything! Lion, lion, come at once! The twos are all ready to march into the ark, and your lioness is waiting. Come at once.'

But usually Shem had to go and find him and drag him to the ark. It was a great nuisance because it kept all the other animals waiting.

Now, this happened night after night, and Mr Noah got very tired of it.

'If you don't come when you're called tonight, lion,

we shall march into the ark without you, and you will be shut out!' he said firmly.

They won't dare to go without me, thought the lion to himself. *I shall keep them waiting as long as I please! Am I not the king of them all?*

That night he sat himself down by the warm fire, curled his tail round him like a cat, and looked down his nose at the bears playing kiss-in-the-ring nearby.

When the time came Mr Noah called to the animals. 'Come to the ark! Line up in twos! It is time to go back.'

All the animals and birds at once stopped their play and ran to the ark. The kangaroos were first. They stood at the head, and after them came the white bears, and then the brown bears, and then the ducks, and then the giraffes, and then, all by herself, the lioness. The lion was missing as usual. The line stretched out in twos, and ended with the elephants, who had been playing hide-and-seek, and had had to scramble out of the coal scuttle to get to the ark.

Mr Noah saw that the lion was missing. But he said nothing. He didn't even look around to see where the lion was. He didn't tell Shem to go and get him. He just said, 'Shem, open the door. Ham, see that the elephants don't tread on the pigs. Japheth, tell the dogs to stop barking. Mrs Noah, would you be good enough to lead the way in?'

Mrs Noah led the way. The animals went in two by two, except the lioness, who went in by herself. Ham scolded the elephants because they trod on the pigs' tails.

Mr Noah went in last. He shut the door with a bang. Everyone settled down in the ark. Not a sound was to be heard.

Now, the lion was rather astonished to see that all the animals had gone in without him. But he didn't say a word or even move from the hearth rug where he sat warming himself.

'I shall stay out as long as I like,' he said to himself grandly. He looked around and saw that all the other toys were going into the toy cupboard. The soldier and the dolls and the teddy bear always came out to play at night too. But now they were settling down quietly.

The soldier was surprised to see the lion on the hearth rug. 'Aren't you going to get into the ark?' he asked. 'Won't you be frightened out here all alone?'

'Frightened!' said the lion, turning up his nose. 'Me, frightened! Don't you know I am the king of all the beasts, and as brave as can be? What should frighten *me* I should like to know?'

'Well, if you feel as grand as all that, you can do what you like!' said the soldier in a huff. 'I'm sure I don't care, Mr High-and-Mighty!'

He got into the toy cupboard and slammed the door. The lion was now all alone. He sat on the rug and blinked at the fire. There was hardly any red coal left. It would soon be out. The nursery was dark, but the lion could see quite well. He had eyes like a cat.

He sat there, and he sat there. Suddenly he heard a scratching noise in the wall nearby. He jumped to his feet. Whatever could it be?

It was the little brown mouse who lived behind the wall. He was coming out of his hole to see if the children had left any crumbs on the floor. He sidled out of the hole and ran over the hearth rug. He bumped into the lion and knocked him over.

'Don't!' said the lion. The mouse stared at him and grinned. He ran at the lion and knocked him over again.

'I said "Don't!"' said the lion in his grandest voice.

'Well, you're sitting on a crumb,' said the mouse. 'Get off it. I want to eat it.'

The lion sat down on the crumb and wouldn't move. He felt very angry with the mouse.

'I wonder if *you* are good to eat!' said the mouse suddenly. 'Do you mind if I nibble your tail?'

'Yes, I do mind,' said the lion, scared. The mouse tried to get the lion's tail in his mouth and the lion ran away. The mouse chased him. Aha! This was fun!

'I'll get your tail!' squeaked the mouse. 'I'll get it!'

The lion ran to the ark and knocked at the door. 'Let me in! A mouse is chasing me.'

'The door is locked,' said Mr Noah. 'Do not wake us up.'

The lion ran to the toy cupboard, and knocked there. 'Let me in!' he cried. 'A mouse is chasing me!'

'Go away,' said the soldier sleepily. 'Do not wake us.'

Well, the lion would certainly have had his tail nibbled if someone hadn't come into the nursery on velvet paws, and scared the mouse away. And that someone was the big tabby cat! She had smelt the mouse and had come after him.

The mouse shot into his hole. The cat saw the lion running and thought he must be a mouse too. So she went after him, and at last she caught him. She pushed him over and sniffed at him. He was very frightened. He felt sure she would eat him.

'You smell strange,' said the cat. 'Very strange. You smell of wood and paint. I will not eat you – but I will play with you.'

She began to push the poor lion about and throw him up into the air. He ran away as fast as he could and once more banged at the door of the ark.

'Let me in, let me in!' he cried. 'A cat is after me.'

'The door is locked,' said Mr Noah. 'Do not wake us up.'

Then the lion ran to the toy cupboard and knocked there again. 'Let me in!' he cried. 'A cat is after me.'

'Go away,' said the soldier sleepily. 'Do not wake us.'

The poor lion was quite in despair – and then he suddenly saw the cat running out of the door. She had heard a mouse downstairs! She was gone.

The lion sat down in front of the fire again, tired and miserable. How he wished he was safely in the ark with all the others! As he sat there a big spider ran over the rug and made him jump!

'Whatever's this now?' cried the lion. 'Go away, whatever you are!'

'I'm going to spin a web from your nose to the leg of the chair,' said the spider. 'Keep still!'

The lion gave a scream and ran away. He knew it was no use going to the ark. He knew it was no use going to the toy cupboard either. Where could he go?

What about the doll's house? he thought. *Yes, the door of that may not be locked!*

He ran to it. He pushed the front door. It opened! The lion slipped inside, shut the door and went into the kitchen. He sat down in a chair there and sighed. At last he was safe!

He didn't feel brave now. He didn't feel like a king. He just felt very small and lonely and frightened.

Katie found the lion in the doll's house the next day, and how surprised she was! *How did he get there?* she wondered. *What a funny thing!*

She put him back into the ark. And that night, when the ark animals clambered out of the ark the lion went too, but he didn't go and sit on the hearth rug alone, looking haughty and grand. No, he mixed with the others and played touch-me-last and hide-and-seek!

And when Mr Noah called the animals to him, who was the first one to come? Yes, the lion! He wasn't going to be locked out again! He had had enough of being grand and mighty. He just wanted to be a good little wooden animal now, ready to go into the ark with the others.

The lioness teases him sometimes. She says, 'Who spent the night in the doll's house like a doll?' And then the lion blushes red all over and doesn't say a word!

Silly Simon and the Goat

Silly Simon and the Goat

SIMON HAD had a cold and his ears had ached. He had been very miserable. Now he was better and up again, but he was rather deaf. That was horrid.

'You'll be able to go to school again tomorrow,' said his mother. 'That will be nice for you. Today you can stay at home and help me.'

So Simon helped his mother. He fetched in the washing from the line. He ran to the shop to get some butter, and he took the baby out for a little walk. He really was a great help.

'You have been quite a sensible boy for once,' said his mother, pleased. Silly Simon wasn't always sensible. He sometimes did very silly things, and then his mother was cross.

He was pleased. 'Well, you always think I haven't got brains,' he said. 'But I have, Mother. I'm really a very clever boy.'

'Well, I hope you go on being a clever boy for the rest of the day,' said his mother. 'Now, I'm going upstairs to do some things. Baby is fast asleep.'

She went upstairs, and then she remembered that she wanted her old coat to mend. So she called down to Simon.

'Simon! Fetch me the old coat, will you?'

Simon didn't hear her very well. He thought his mother said, 'Fetch me the old goat.' He was rather surprised, but still, as he was feeling very good and obedient, he set off to fetch the old goat in from the field.

He caught the goat, and led him to the house on a rope. He called up to his mother. 'I've got it for you.'

'Well, bring it upstairs, and hang it over the banisters,' called his mother. Simon felt more astonished than before. It was funny to want the old goat brought into the house, but still stranger to want it upstairs hung over the banisters.

'That goat won't like it!' he called up after a bit. But his mother only half heard what he said.

'Don't be silly!' she said. 'It won't hurt the coat. But hang it in the hall, if you'd rather.'

'Hang you in the hall?' said Simon to the surprised goat. 'Which would you rather, goat? I can hang you in the hall, or take you upstairs and put you over the banisters.'

The goat didn't seem to mind which. So Simon took it into the hall and looked at the pegs there. He tried to tie the rope to a peg, but the goat broke away at once, pulling the peg rack down with a crash.

'Simon!' shouted his mother crossly. 'What in the world are you doing? Be quiet.'

'There!' said Simon to the goat. 'You'll be getting

into trouble if you make noises like that. You'd better come upstairs. I think it would be easier to put you over the banisters, after all.'

So the goat was dragged upstairs. It made a great noise and Simon's mother called out again.

'You'll wake the baby! What are you making all that noise for?'

'I'm dragging the goat up,' panted Simon. 'It won't come.'

'A coat isn't as heavy as all that,' said his mother crossly. 'What a fuss you make to be sure! I hope you're not dragging it on the floor.'

Simon at last got the goat to the top of the stairs. He tried to get it across the banisters, but the goat simply wouldn't go. As fast as Simon lifted it up one end it slipped to the ground the other end. It was a most annoying goat.

'Simon! Whatever are you doing out there?' called his mother. 'Why can't you be quiet?'

'There!' said Simon to the goat fiercely. 'You'll

get me into trouble if you don't behave. Now just you let me put you across the banisters!'

But it was no good. The goat wouldn't be at all helpful. It clattered with its four feet, it slid here and there, and was altogether most obstinate.

It suddenly got very tired of Simon. It backed a little way, put its head down, ran at Simon and caught him full on its head. It butted him hard, and Simon rose in the air with a yell, sailed down the stairs, and landed at the bottom with a crash. He howled loudly. The baby woke up and yelled too.

Simon's mother flung open the door to glare at Simon – but instead she found herself glaring at the old goat, who glared back, and looked as if he might butt her at any moment. Simon's mother hurriedly stepped back into the room and shut the door.

She called through it. 'You bad boy, Simon! How dare you bring that old goat up here? Take him back to the field at once!'

'Well, you told me to bring him here and hang him

over the banisters,' wailed Simon. 'You did, you did!'

'Oh! Oh, you foolish, silly, stupid boy!' cried his mother. 'I told you to fetch my old coat – I wanted to mend it! Oh, why did I ever say you were good and sensible today?'

The goat trotted neatly downstairs and into the hall. It went into the kitchen and out of the back door. It had had enough of Simon and Simon's mother and the crying baby.

'It's gone!' said Simon. 'But, oh, Mother, it's taken a rug with it to eat!'

'Oh, has it?' cried his mother, and shot out of the room and downstairs to catch the goat. But she was too late. The goat had eaten the rug.

Then Simon got sent up to his room, and he was very upset about it.

'I try to be good and sensible and obedient and this is what I get for it!' he wept. 'I'll never try again.'

'Well, if you do things like that when you are trying to be good, you'd better stop!' said his mother.

Poor Simon! You wouldn't think anyone would be so silly, would you?

The Very Little Hen

The Very Little Hen

THERE WAS once a fine fat hen called Chucky, who laid beautiful brown eggs every single day. She belonged to Dame See-Saw, and was one of a big flock, for the old dame made her living selling eggs.

Now, one day Chucky wandered out of the old woman's garden. She knew she ought not to do this, for she had often been warned that the world outside was not good for hens. But the gate was open and out she walked.

She hadn't gone very far before she met Ten-Toes the pixie.

'Good morning,' he said. 'Come here, my dear, and

let me see what sort of an egg you can lay for my dinner. I'm very hungry indeed, and a nice boiled egg would do me a lot of good!'

So Chucky laid him an egg. It was one of her very best, big and brown, and Ten-Toes was very pleased. He made himself a fire, put his little saucepan on to boil, and very soon the egg was in the bubbling water. Ten-Toes ate it with a crust of bread, and said that it was the nicest he had ever tasted.

'You must come home with me,' he said to Chucky. 'I'd like an egg like that every day.'

'Oh, I can't come with you,' said Chucky, frightened. 'I belong to Dame See-Saw. I must go back.'

'No, no,' said Ten-Toes, and he picked up the fat brown hen. But she struggled so hard and pecked his finger so badly that he grew angry.

'Ho, ho!' he said in a nasty voice. 'So you think you won't come with me, do you? Well, I'll soon show you that you're wrong.'

With that he tapped Chucky on the head with his

wand and said two magic words. In a second the hen grew much, much smaller – so small that she was no bigger than a buttercup flower!

'Ha!' said Ten-Toes. 'Now you can peck all you like, but you won't be able to hurt me! And when I get you home, I'll change you back to your right size again, and make you lay me an egg every day!'

But when Chucky heard that, she fled off between the blades of grass, clucking loudly in fear. At first she didn't know what had happened to her, but soon she guessed that she had been made very, very small, for the grass towered above her, and the face of a daisy seemed as big as the sun!

She made her way back to Dame See-Saw and told her all that had happened!

But Dame See-Saw was cross. 'What use are you to me now, I'd like to know?' she cried. 'I can't turn you back to your right size again, and all the other hens will peck you. The eggs you lay will be so tiny that I shan't be able to sell them. You can just walk out of the garden gate again, and go to seek your living somewhere else!'

Poor Chucky! She ran out of the gate, clucking in despair. Who would have her now that she was so small?

I'll go to Tweedle the gnome, she thought. *He isn't very big. Perhaps he'd like to keep me.*

But Tweedle laughed when he saw Chucky.

'What good would your eggs be to me?' he asked. 'Why, I could put twenty in my mouth at once and not know they were there! No, I don't want you, Chucky.'

Then the little hen went to the goblins in the hill, though she was really rather afraid of them. But they didn't like eggs.

'We never eat them,' they said. 'And we couldn't sell them, Chucky, because they are so very tiny. No, we don't want you, Chucky.'

Chucky wandered off to the Wise Man, and begged him to keep her, and she would lay him eggs every day.

'But what could I do with them?' asked the Wise Man. 'They're so small that I should have to put on my biggest pair of spectacles to see them. No, Chucky, I don't want you!'

Poor Chucky went away sadly. Nobody wanted her. There wasn't any room for her anywhere. She went on and on until at last she came to a beautiful garden. In one corner of it was built a playhouse for the children, and in this they kept all their toys.

There was a rocking horse, a big shelf full of books, a toy fort, a Noah's ark, two dolls, a toy clown, a teddy bear, a box of tricks and, last of all, a lovely toy farm. The little hen peeped in at the door and thought it was a lovely place. She wondered if there was anyone there who would like to have her for their own.

But Peter and Jane, who owned the lovely playhouse, were not there. They were staying at their granny's so the toys were all alone. They saw the tiny hen at the door and called to her to come in.

'What a little mite!' they cried. 'Are you alive or are you a toy like us?'

'I'm alive,' said Chucky, and she told the toys her story, and how she could find nowhere to live. Then the toys all began to talk at once, and there was a tremendous noise. At last the teddy bear held up his hand for silence, and everyone was still.

'Chucky,' said the teddy bear to the tiny hen, 'would you like to come and live with us here? There is a toy farm over there, with sheep, cows, horses, goats, pigs, ducks and one cockerel. There used to be a hen too, but she got broken. The cockerel is lonely, and as he is just about your size, we are sure he would be delighted to welcome you to his little shed.'

Chucky was so happy that she could hardly speak. She looked at the little toy farm and thought it was the prettiest place she had ever seen. It was all fenced round, and the farm stood in the middle with the barns and sheds here and there. The farmer and his wife, both made of wood, waved to Chucky.

She ran to them, and they bent down and stroked her. She was just the right size for them. Then the little wooden cockerel strutted up and admired Chucky. His feathers were only painted on, but Chucky's were real, and he thought she was wonderful.

'Welcome to my shed!' he said, and he led Chucky to the door of a tiny shed nearby.

'I think I'll lay the farmer an egg to show how grateful I am,' said Chucky, and she straight away laid a beautiful brown egg in the little nesting box there. How delighted the farmer and his wife were! All the toys crowded round to see it too!

'Well, the hen that got broken never laid an egg in her life!' cried the farmer's wife. 'What a clever little thing you are, to be sure!'

'Let's have some baby chickens!' cried the farmer. 'We won't eat your eggs yet, Chucky. Lay a dozen in the nesting box, and then sit on them. It would be grand to have twelve yellow chicks running about the farm!'

So Chucky laid twelve brown eggs, and sat on them – and, do you know, one morning they all hatched out into the tiniest, prettiest yellow chicks you ever saw! Chucky and everyone else were so proud of them! It made the toy farm seem quite real to have the little chicks running about everywhere.

Tomorrow Peter and Jane are coming back from their granny's – and whatever will they say when they see the little chicks, each no bigger than a pea, racing about the toy farm, cheeping loudly? I really can't think!

As for Chucky, she has quite forgotten what it was like to be a great big hen. She is happy as the day is long, trotting about with her chicks on the little toy farm.

Spiny's Good Turn

Spiny's Good Turn

JEAN LOVED her little garden. She had two patches. In one she grew flowers and in the other she grew radishes and lettuces for tea.

She really loved taking in a nice fresh lettuce and a dozen radishes to her mother, so that the family could eat them with bread and butter and salt for tea. But this year Jean wasn't having much luck with her garden.

First something ate her seedlings, and she had to plant them again. Then something ate her lettuces.

'I'm afraid it's rabbits, darling,' said her mother. 'What a nuisance! I don't know why they should choose your bit of garden to nibble at. Never mind – we'll get Daddy to put some wire netting round your two patches, then your plants will be safe.'

Well, they were safe from the rabbits – but then something else came to eat the little seedlings and the lettuces, and to gnaw nasty little places in the tender young radishes!

'What is eating my things now?' said Jean, upset. 'It's too bad! I'll never be able to bring you flowers or lettuces or radishes this summer, Mummy!'

'It's slugs, dear,' said her mother. 'And these nasty little caterpillars. You really are unfortunate!'

Now, as Jean went down to her garden the next day, she saw something moving in the hedge. She went to look, and found a little prickly hedgehog caught in a piece of barbed wire there. 'Oh dear! Poor little thing,' said Jean, 'you've hurt your leg!'

She carried the prickly hedgehog in her hanky and went indoors to her mother. They unwrapped it and looked at it. It immediately curled itself up into a tight, spiny ball – but the hurt leg hung out, torn and bleeding.

'Poor little creature,' said Mother. 'I'll put some antiseptic on its leg and bind it up.'

So she did. But when it uncurled itself it could hardly walk. 'What shall we do with it?' said Jean.

'We must put it somewhere safe for a little while,' said her mother. 'I know! We'll put it on your garden patch, Jean – the wire netting will keep it safe there till its leg is better. We'll feed it each day.'

'Won't it eat my plants?' asked Jean.

'Oh, no. Hedgehogs won't touch those,' said Mother. 'Look, you carry him there in your hanky, and I'll bring a saucer of food out.'

Soon the hedgehog was safely in the wire-enclosed patch. He lay there, curled up tightly, his bandaged leg sticking out of his spines. Jean's mother put down a saucer of dog food. In a few minutes the hedgehog uncurled, smelt the dog food, and dragged himself over to it. He ate it eagerly, taking the pieces into his mouth hungrily.

'I like him,' said Jean. 'I shall call him Spiny. He's nice. Mummy, look at his funny little snout and his bright, beady eyes. He's looking at me!'

Spiny stayed in the patch for four whole days! He seemed perfectly happy. His leg healed well, and he could soon use it quite easily.

And then Jean noticed something. Her lettuces had grown big and strong. Her radishes were almost ready to eat. Her seedlings hadn't been eaten by slugs or grubs! *How marvellous!* thought Jean.

'Mummy – it's Spiny that has eaten up every grub and caterpillar and slug!' she said in surprise. 'I watched him today, snuffling under a lettuce – and he brought out a big fat slug and gobbled it up!'

'Well, fancy even a little hedgehog repaying a good turn!' said Mother. 'Who would have thought it?'

Jean was quite right. The hedgehog had looked for grubs and caterpillars and had gobbled up every one he found! No wonder the lettuces and radishes grew well.

'I do wish Spiny would stay in our garden,' said Jean. 'He would be so useful. I'd like to have a hedgehog for a pet. But I expect he'll wander away as soon as I set him free.'

'Well, he can't stay in your little wired-up patch now that his leg is better,' said her mother. 'He's a wild animal and we must set him free.'

So they set him free – but, do you know, Spiny didn't wander away! He liked Jean and he liked the garden. So he stayed, and made himself into a pet. How do I know all this?

Well, you see, I went to tea with Jean the other day and had fine red radishes and crisp green lettuce out of her garden. She told me about Spiny, of course, and I went to see him. Isn't she lucky to have a hedgehog to eat all her slugs?

What a Surprise!

What a Surprise!

BARRY WAS very fond of birds, and every morning he put out crumbs for them, and a saucer of fresh water. He made a bird table too – just a piece of wood on the top of a pole – and from it he hung strings of unshelled peanuts that he had carefully threaded together, and a coconut with a hole made at each end. He put all kinds of titbits on the table, and you should have seen the birds that came to visit it!

When Barry's birthday came, the postman knocked at the door and left three parcels, a small one and two big ones. Inside the small one was a silver pencil – and inside the two big ones were wooden nesting boxes to put up in the garden for the birds to nest in! Barry was so pleased.

'Just what I've always wanted!' he said, looking at the two boxes in delight. They were very nicely made, and the top part, which made a slanting roof, could be lifted up – so that Barry would be able to peep inside and see if any bird had begun to nest there.

'I shall put these nesting boxes up today,' said the little boy. 'I shall put one in the chestnut tree – I know a fine place there – and one I shall fasten among the rose ramblers. There is such a small hole in each for the birds to get in and out that I am sure only the tiny tits will make their homes there. What fun it will be!'

So out he went very happily into the garden, and soon the two nesting boxes were in their places. One was well hidden among the ramblers and the other was neatly hung on the trunk of a small chestnut tree, protected by an overhanging branch.

'If I were you, Barry,' said his mother, 'I would

hang up bits of fat or peanuts near your new nesting boxes, and then, when the tits come to them, they will see the boxes and perhaps think they are good nesting places.'

So Barry hung a few peanuts by each box, and begged a piece of suet to hang up too. In ten minutes' time the tits had found the nuts and the suet, and were very busily pecking away at them. Barry could hear them calling to one another in excitement.

'This is suet, this is, this is suet, this is! Peanuts, peanuts, peanuts! This is suet!'

The tits were pleased to find more food in the garden. They thought that Barry was the nicest, kindest boy in the world, and they were always happy in his garden. One of them flew to the top of a nesting box. He wondered what it was – it hadn't been there before. He hopped about all over it, sometimes the right way up, sometimes upside down. He didn't really mind whether he swung one way or another!

Then he called to his wife, 'Come and see!'

She flew down to him. 'Look!' said the tit in excitement. 'There is a little hole here. It leads into a nice dark room. Let us go inside and see whether it would be a good place to nest in.'

So in they went, and they both decided that it would be exactly right. This was the box that Barry had put in the rose ramblers. The other box was taken by another pair of excited tits, who were most delighted to find such a fine nesting place.

'It's near plenty of food!' they sang. 'It's in the garden of the nicest boy in the world! There are no cats! We shall be safe, safe, safe!'

Then they began to build their cosy nests. They made them of the softest things they could find – bits of moss taken from the ditch, a great many hairs from the post against which the brown horses in the field rubbed themselves each day. And some hairs from the dog next door. When he shook himself a few hairs flew from his coat, and the tits were always on the watch for these. They would hunt about the lawn for them.

Then they lined their nests with soft feathers. Some they found in the hen run, and how they squabbled with the sparrows over them! The sparrows liked the feathers too, to make a lining for their nests, and tried their best to take them all – but the tits pounced down in a flash, and carried off most of the downy feathers under the very beaks of the angry sparrows!

The nest of the tits in the rose rambler box was finished first. It was so cosy and warm. Barry knew that they were building there, for he watched them carrying moss and hair in their beaks to the ramblers. He was delighted. One day, when he knew that both the tits had left the nest, he went quietly to it and lifted up the roof lid. He gazed inside before he shut down the lid, and to his great delight saw five pretty little eggs. Now there would be crowds of fluffy yellow baby tits calling all over the garden to their parents!

He ran indoors to tell his mother.

'I'm so glad,' she said. 'But if I were you, Barry, I wouldn't peep inside any more. The tits may not like it, and it would be so dreadful if you made them desert their nest and leave their eggs or young ones. It does sometimes happen, you know.'

So Barry did not go and peep any more. When he did the next time he got a great surprise, as you will hear.

Now, as you probably know, all birds and animals can see the little folk, although very few humans can do so. The tits especially are friendly with them, for the fairies love the merry, pretty little birds, with their bright voices and amusing ways.

Very often the tits went to the woods nearby where many elves lived, and in their hunt for small insects they came across many of the little folk and talked to them. And one day the tits that nested in the rose rambler box found an elf of great use to them.

She lived in a hole at the foot of an old oak tree. The two tits often went to hunt for insects in the bark and the elf liked their merry voices, and always popped her little golden head out to wish them good day.

One morning the tits were hunting in the oak tree bark when a gun went off not far away. It was the farmer shooting rabbits. It frightened the tits so much that they rose straight up into the air to fly – and one of them flew full tilt into the branch overhead and hurt himself so badly that he fell down to the ground in a faint, his eyes closed, and his wings drooping.

'What's the matter, what's the matter?' called his little wife in a fright. She flew down to her mate, but he did not move. Then she heard a scampering of feet not far off and saw the bright-eyed weasel, whom all small creatures and birds fear, for he feasts on them.

'Help! Help!' cried the little tit in a panic, and she flew up into the air. The weasel stopped – and then came running over to the oak tree.

But before he could snap up the poor little tit

someone came rushing out of the roots of the oak. It was the golden-headed elf. She caught up the tiny tit and ran back with him into her home. He was safe there, for the weasel could not possibly squeeze into the small hole where she lived.

'I'll pay you out for that!' he shouted at her and ran off, mad with rage, for he was hungry.

In a few minutes the tit opened his eyes and stretched his wings, none the worse for his bump. When he found the elf bending over him, and heard what had happened, he was very grateful indeed.

'It is most kind of you!' he said in his shrill little voice. 'Most kind indeed! Let me know, elf, if you want help yourself at any time, and my wife and I will be very pleased to do whatever we can for you!'

Then he flew to his wife back at their nest in the box, where he rested all day and was soon quite himself again. When their eggs hatched out into five pretty little youngsters the two tits were mad with delight. They sang about them until everyone in the garden was quite tired of hearing how beautiful and how marvellous the baby tits were. But indeed they really were very sweet, for they were just bundles of blue and yellow fluff.

One day the robin brought a message to the two tits.

'Bluetits!' he sang, 'I bring a message to you from the elf in the woods. She is very unhappy and asks you to go to her.'

Off went the tits at once. The elf was not in her usual place under the oak tree – but they found her shivering in the ditch not far away, with only a cobweb shawl wrapped round her.

'What is wrong?' cried the tits, flying down beside her.

'Oh, little friends,' said the elf, 'a dreadful thing has happened to me. The weasel was so angry because I saved the life of one of you the other day that he said he would force me to go away. He sent an army of red ants into my cosy home and they ate up all my pretty clothes, and bit me so hard that I could not stay there any more. Now they are building their nest in the oak tree roots, so I have no home. I don't know where to go, because if I choose another hole the ants will come after me there too. Now here I am, cold and hungry in this ditch, with only this cobweb shawl to keep me warm. I am so dreadfully afraid that the weasel will come after me.'

'You poor little thing!' cried the tits, cuddling close to her. 'What can we do for you? Let us think hard!'

So they thought very hard, and then the little hen tit cried out in delight.

'I know! I know! Let the elf come to live with us in our nesting box! It is true that we are rather crowded now that we have five babies – but it is warm and cosy, and the elf will have plenty of company and be quite safe from the weasel there!'

'Oh, that would be wonderful!' said the elf, tears of joy coming into her eyes. 'Oh, there is nothing in the world that I would like better! I could look after the babies for you when you went out together, couldn't I?'

'Yes, you could!' cried both tits, delighted. 'There is one of our children who is far too bold. We are afraid he will climb out of the little entrance hole one day and fall to the ground. Then the weasel will be sure to get him. If *you* were living in the nest with us we should never be afraid of leaving the babies alone. Do come!'

The elf spread her pretty gleaming wings, and flew up into the air with the tits. The weasel, who was hiding in the bushes not far off, gave a snicker of rage. He had been hoping to pounce on the elf that very day.

The tits took the elf to their nesting box. She was just too big to squeeze in through the little hole, so she had to lift up the roof and get in that way. She cuddled down among the fluffy babies and was soon as warm as toast.

How happy she was there! And how pleased all the seven tits were to have her! She was so good to them all. She looked after the five babies carefully when the two parents were away, and wouldn't let the bold one try to climb out of the hole. She saw that each baby had his share of the food in turn, and would not let the strong ones rob the weak ones. She brushed their feathers and told them tales. They loved her very much indeed.

She was warm and cosy there, and had plenty to eat, for the little tits brought her all kinds of food each day. They knew which flowers had the sweetest honey, and they were very clever at bringing leaves with dewdrops on them, so that the elf could drink. Nobody knew that the elf lived in the box, not even the other tits. It was a secret.

And then somebody found out. Guess who it was! Yes, it was Barry. He did so badly want to see how many baby birds the tits had in the rose rambler box. So one sunny morning he tiptoed to it, after he had seen the tit parents fly out, and he lifted up the roof lid to see inside.

He looked down – and there, looking up at him, were five fluffy blue and yellow baby tits – and one pretty golden-headed elf! She was cuddled down among the tits, her arms round them, the prettiest sight you could imagine!

Barry was so surprised that he simply stood and stared. Then he quietly closed the lid and went away. It was the greatest and loveliest surprise of his life – a real secret that he couldn't tell to anyone at all.

When the parent birds came back the elf told them what had happened. She was frightened. 'I must fly off!' she said. 'That boy will come back and take me away.'

'No, no,' sang the tits at once. 'Don't be afraid of Barry. He is the nicest boy in the world! He would not harm us, and he will not harm you. You are quite safe here. Let him peep at you if he wants to. He will never, never hurt you!'

When the five baby tits flew away into the garden in the bright summertime, the elf stayed in the nesting box and made it her home. She tidied it up, and she made a small cupboard for herself and a shelf where she put all her belongings.

'Do come back and nest here next year,' she begged the tits, who often came and peeped in at the hole to talk to her.

'We will!' they promised. 'We certainly will!'

So there the elf still lives, as Barry knows very well! He peeps at her once a week, and she knows him well now and smiles gaily at him. He has never told anyone his great secret – but I know because the tits told the robin and he sang it all to me! And how I'd love to go and peep in that box – wouldn't you?

The Old Toad and the Spider

The Old Toad and the Spider

THERE WAS once a sly old toad who lived in a damp ditch at the bottom of a large garden. Each spring he crawled to the nearby pond and played with the other toads there. When he was tired of that he went back to his ditch to wait for flies and caterpillars to come along for his dinner.

One summer his ditch dried up, and the toad felt hot and uncomfortable. So he left the ditch and crawled through the hedge.

Soon he came to an orchard, where the leaves of the trees threw a thick green shade. The grass below was long and wet. The toad liked it. It felt cool to his brown back and he liked the wetness. He sat beneath an apple tree and waited for flies.

'There are plenty in this orchard,' said the toad to himself. 'I shall grow fat and comfortable.'

Now, just above him lived a spider. She was old and big and cunning. She had spun more webs than she could remember, and had caught thousands of flies. She was not pleased when she saw the toad.

'The tiresome old creature!' she said to herself. 'This is the best place in the whole orchard for flies. That is why I have made my web here. It is *my* place, not his.'

So she spoke to the old toad from her place in the middle of the web.

'Toad! You must find another hunting ground. I have spun my web here every summer for years!'

The toad blinked up at her with his beautiful coppery eyes. 'I shall stay here,' he said. 'There are flies enough for both.'

The spider watched him. A large bluebottle came

by and the toad sat as still as a stone. The bluebottle settled on a grass at the edge of the spider's web – but before the spider could dart on it the toad shot out his long sticky tongue, hit the fly with the end of it, and drew it quickly into his mouth! He swallowed, blinked – and the fly was gone!

'*Very* nice!' said the toad. '*Much* better than going to the trouble of making a web! My tongue is fastened to the front of my mouth instead of to the back, so I can fling it out quite a long way. That was a most tasty bluebottle, spider.'

The spider was very angry. She saw the toad catch fly after fly with his quick tongue, and only a few of the smaller ones came into her web.

Then came two or three wet days, and no flies were about. The toad grew very hungry. The spider saw that he was thinner and she spoke to him.

'Toad, do you like the water? From where I swing in my web I can see the pond, and there are all kinds of flies hovering over the surface. Why do you not go and catch a few till the weather becomes warm again?'

The toad knew that many flies hovered over the pond in the summer. He thought about it. Then slowly he crawled away to the pond. The spider was delighted. She knew something that the toad did not know. She knew that the white ducks came to the pond every day for a swim.

'They will eat the toad!' she said. 'That will be the end of him. Then I shall be able to catch all the orchard flies myself.'

The toad came to the pond. He went in with a flop. He swam about gracefully, enjoying the water. The spider had spoken truthfully, for there were a great many flies skimming the top of the water. The toad ate as many as he wanted.

It was friendly of the spider to tell me, he thought. But he quite changed his mind when midday came. For then the eight white ducks came too, quacking and waddling, longing for their swim! They flopped into the water and paddled their legs so that they swam all about. Some of them put their heads down to see what they could find below the surface. The toad was most alarmed.

He swam quickly to a rock he knew, and squeezed himself under it. But a duck had seen him and came probing under the rock with her beak. The toad only just got out at the other side in time. He swam to the side of the pond and crawled into a mass of rushes. But when the ducks came waddling round that side he had to jump into the water again and swim all the way across the pond in a great hurry.

He crawled out, very tired. He was angry with the spider, very angry indeed. He knew she had played a trick on him. He made his way back to the orchard, meaning to break her web and eat her.

But the spider was watching for him. She curled herself up, with her eight legs beneath her, and lay as if she were dead under a piece of loose bark near her web.

The toad lumbered up, his copper eyes gleaming.

He put up a paw and broke the lovely web. Then he looked for the spider. When he found her, lying on her back looking as dead as could be, he gave a croak.

'Dead! Ha, and a good thing too! Serve her right for playing me such a trick! Well, I don't eat dead spiders, so I'll leave her there for the field mice to eat.'

He went to find himself a good stone to crawl beneath, because the nights were growing a little chilly and he knew that soon the time would come when he must sleep for the winter. He must have a good stone then, or he might be found and eaten by some hungry animal.

As soon as he had gone, the spider came alive again, in the quick way that spiders have. Her legs straightened out, and she stood the right way up, her big eyes looking all around her. She saw the toad crawling under a stone.

She ran over to it. Above were twigs, and quickly the spider wove a big web just above the stone.

So, when the toad crawled out into the sun to catch a few autumn flies, he found the spider in the middle of a big web just above him.

'But you were dead!' he croaked in surprise and dismay.

'Not really!' said the spider, and she swung to and fro in her web. 'Not really!'

And now the cold days are coming when the toad and spider will sleep. You will find the spider crouching as if she were dead behind a loose piece of bark – and the toad will be asleep under his stone! Don't disturb them, for they are good friends of ours. In the spring they will wake again and try their tricks on one another. Who do you suppose will win?

Binkle's Tail

Binkle's Tail

ONCE THERE was a guinea pig called Binkle. He lived in a cage just outside Jinky the gnome's front door, and he was very proud of himself.

'My whiskers are fine, my fur is soft, and my ears are pretty!' he said to himself. 'No wonder all Jinky's visitors come and talk to me!'

But one day Panikin the pixie said something that gave Binkle a terrible fright.

'Whatever you do, Jinky, don't let anyone hold Binkle up by his tail. If you do, his eyes will fall out!' he said solemnly.

'Oh! Oh! Oh!' squeaked poor Binkle, hiding

himself in a corner. 'I do hope nobody would do such a cruel thing!'

Jinky the gnome and Panikin the pixie laughed loudly and Binkle couldn't think what they were laughing at. When they had gone he began thinking very hard.

Just suppose someone did come and hold me up by my tail! he thought. *How terrible it would be! I wonder what my tail is like?* He tried to see it, but he was such a plump little guinea pig that he couldn't see anything beyond his humpy back.

'It must be rather a long tail,' he said sadly. 'Perhaps Panikin was afraid some rude person would swing me upside down by it. Oh dear! What shall I do?'

The more he thought about it, the more he felt afraid. At last he decided to run away that night, go to Snip the tailor, and ask him to cut his tail right off. *Then no one can hold me up by it!* thought Binkle.

So that night, out he scampered and ran down the road to Snip the tailor.

Snip was sitting making a coat for a brownie. 'Hello!' he said in surprise. 'What do you want, Binkle?'

'Please would you cut my tail off?' begged Binkle. 'I'm afraid someone will hold me up by it, and then my eyes would drop out, you know.'

Snip stared at him, and smiled. 'I'm terribly sorry,' he said, 'but I'm afraid my scissors couldn't cut off your tail; they're not the right sort. Go and ask Periwinkle the dressmaker. She's got a pair of brand-new scissors!'

'Thank you,' said Binkle and off he scampered. As he went he heard Snip laughing, and he couldn't think what he was laughing at. He climbed the hill to Periwinkle's.

'I want my tail cut off, in case someone holds me up by it and makes my eyes fall out,' explained Binkle. 'Snip said you'd got a new pair of scissors.'

'So I have. But I'm afraid they wouldn't cut your tail off, Binkle,' said Periwinkle. 'Go and ask Pippit the draper. He's got lots of scissors there.'

'Thank you,' said Binkle, and ran off as quickly as he could. As he went, he heard Periwinkle laughing, and he couldn't think what she was laughing at.

Pippit the draper was just shutting up shop when Binkle came panting up.

'Why, Binkle!' said Pippit. 'Why are you out so late?'

'I'm dreadfully worried about my tail,' said Binkle. 'If I'm held up by it, my eyes will drop out. Periwinkle said you could cut it off, as you have lots of scissors.'

'So I have,' said Pippit, laughing. 'But they're all much too small. Why don't you go to the Simple Witch down in the valley? She's got a pair of magic scissors.'

Binkle hurried to the witch's cottage, wondering why Pippit had laughed, and asked for her help. 'Pippit said you had some magic scissors. It won't hurt, will it?'

'Oh, no, Binkle, it won't hurt you at all!' chuckled the Simple Witch.

She picked up a pair of big shiny scissors. Binkle turned his back to her and waited nervously. Snip! Snap! he heard, but he felt nothing at all.

'There you are!' said the witch. 'You haven't any tail to worry about now, Binkle!'

'Oh, thank you very much indeed!' said Binkle, and ran home, full of delight.

As he went, he heard the witch laughing and laughing, and he couldn't think what she was laughing at. He cuddled himself up in his little cage, and felt very happy.

Now I'm quite safe, he thought. *My eyes will never drop out. I wonder what Jinky will say. Won't he be pleased to think no one can ever hold me up by my tail!*

Binkle soon fell fast asleep. When he woke the next day he tried to look over his plump shoulder to check that his tail wasn't there. But, of course, he was much too fat.

Just then, Jinky came whistling down the garden. But, dear me, he didn't seem to notice anything new about Binkle at all, and he couldn't think why the little guinea pig kept turning his back on him. 'What's the matter, Binkle?' he asked at last.

'I've had my tail cut off,' said Binkle proudly, 'so that no one can hold me up by it and make my eyes fall out! The Simple Witch did it with her magic scissors!'

To his surprise Jinky began to laugh and laugh, and Binkle couldn't think what he was laughing at. 'What's the matter?' he asked, quite offended.

'Oh, Binkle – hee, hee, hee – it's so funny – ha, ha – you never had a tail at all – ho, ho, ho! Guinea pigs don't have tails, you silly!' Jinky said, laughing loudly.

And then Binkle knew why Snip and Periwinkle, Pippit and the Simple Witch had all laughed so loudly the night before. Poor Binkle!

The Great Big Bumblebee

The Great Big Bumblebee

ONE MORNING LOUISE was playing with her dolls in the nursery when her mother came in.

'What are you playing at, darling?' she asked.

'I'm playing at having a wedding with my dolls,' said Louise. 'But I haven't any white frock nice enough to dress Angelina in, Mummy. She's the bride, you know.'

'Well, if you run upstairs to the attic, and look in the big black trunk near the window, you'll find an old white frock of mine,' said Mother. 'Bring it down, and I'll help you to cut it up and make a lovely wedding dress for Angelina.'

So Louise ran upstairs to the attic, and went to the black trunk. She lifted up the lid and looked inside. There, wrapped in tissue paper, was an old white satin dress of Mother's. Just as Louise was going to lift it out she heard a loud buzzing noise, and looked round to see what it was.

'Goodness, it's a big bumblebee!' she said. 'I've never seen such a big one before! Poor thing, it's got into the attic, and now it can't find the way out.'

The great bee was buzzing up and down the windowpane, and Louise went to look at him. His body was covered with brown and yellow fur, and his wings whirred so quickly that they made the loudest buzzing Louise had ever heard.

'Look! Get out of the space at the top of the window,' said Louise. 'That's where you flew in, bumblebee.'

But the bee didn't understand. It flew up and down the glass, up and down, frightened and unhappy. It wanted to get out into the garden, where there was sunshine and plenty of flowers, and it *couldn't* find the way.

Louise felt sorry for it. She did not like to touch it, for she was much too afraid that it would sting her – but she couldn't leave it there in the attic, buzzing up and down the window all day long.

What can I do for the poor thing? thought Louise. *Perhaps if I got a piece of paper and put it under the bee and then guided it up to the top of the window, it would have the sense to fly out.*

She fetched a piece of paper, and then put it gently below the bumblebee. Her hand trembled, for she really was afraid it might sting her, but she didn't draw back, even when the bee buzzed more loudly than ever.

She pushed it carefully right to the top of the window – then BUZZ! The bee flew right out into the garden, and Louise could hear it no longer. It had gone back to the flowers.

Then the little girl went to the black trunk and

took out the white satin dress she had come to fetch. She carried it downstairs, and soon she and her mother were busy cutting out a lovely wedding dress for Angelina.

It *was* a beauty! They worked hard at it all day long, and then dressed the doll in her new frock after tea. She looked simply lovely.

'Oh, Mummy, could I take Angelina in her wedding dress with me when I go out to tea at Auntie Mary's tomorrow?' asked Louise.

'Yes,' said Mother. 'I'm sure Auntie Mary would like to see her.'

So next day, when it was time to start out for her auntie's house, and Louise was washed and dressed in her blue cotton dress, she picked up Angelina, and carried her with her.

'It's a good thing it has stopped raining,' said Mother, 'or Angelina might have got wet. The sun is shining now, so you will be all right. Don't tread in the puddles, darling!'

Off went Louise, carrying Angelina in her lovely new wedding dress. She *was* glad the rain had stopped.

Just as Louise had gone halfway to her Auntie Mary's house, a big dog came running up, splashing through all the puddles. He ran straight to Louise and sniffed at her legs.

'Go away,' said Louise, holding Angelina out of his reach. 'You're treading on my shoes with your muddy paws. Go away!'

Suddenly the dog jumped up at the doll, and tried to snatch it from Louise. His muddy paws left a dirty mark on the doll's new dress, and Louise was very upset.

'Oh, *do* go away!' she said to the dog. 'Stop jumping up at Angelina.'

But the dog wouldn't stop. He thought Louise was having a game with him, and he meant to get Angelina and chew her up. Louise was in despair. Whatever could she do to make him stop? There was nobody nearby at all who could help. The dog jumped higher, and Louise felt certain that he would soon get her doll.

Then suddenly there came a loud buzzing sound – and down flew a great big furry bumblebee! He flew straight at the naughty dog and sat on his nose.

'Wuff!' went the dog in fright, for the bee stung him hard.

The bee flew off his nose, circled round Louise's head once or twice and then flew off again. The dog rubbed his nose with his paw, and then, whining loudly, ran off home down the road.

'Oh, fancy that bee helping me like that!' said Louise. 'Why, it must have been the same one that *I* helped yesterday! It looked just as big and beautiful, and it had just as loud a buzz. Oh, I *am* glad I helped it to fly out of the attic window. If I hadn't, it might still be there now, and wouldn't have been able to save Angelina today!'

Off she went to her auntie's, and told her all about her adventure with the dog and the bee.

'That kind big bumblebee saved Angelina from being chewed to pieces,' said Louise. 'I'm *sure* it was the same bee that I helped out of the window, don't you think so, Auntie?'

I think it must have been too – don't you?

The Cat Without Whiskers

The Cat Without Whiskers

INKY WAS a black cat with the finest white whiskers in the street. He was a handsome cat, with sharp ears and a long thick tail that looked like a snake when he waved it to and fro. He had a white mark under his chin, which the children called his bib, and he washed it three times a day, so that it was always like snow.

Inky was plump, for he was the best ratter and mouser in the town and never lacked a good dinner. When he sat on the wall washing himself he was a fine sight, for his glossy fur gleamed in the sun and his whiskers stuck out each side of his face like white wires.

'I'm the finest-looking cat in the town,' said Inky

proudly, and he looked scornfully down at the tabby in the garden below, and the white cat washing itself on a windowsill nearby. 'Nobody is as good-looking as me!'

Then a little boy came by, and when he saw the big black cat sitting up on the wall he shouted up at him, laughing, 'Hello, Whiskers!'

Inky was offended. His name wasn't Whiskers. It was Inky. A little girl heard what the boy said and she laughed. 'That's a good name for him,' she said. 'He's a very whiskery cat. Whiskers!'

Everyone thought it a funny name, and soon Inky was being called Whiskers all day long, even by the cats and dogs around. This made him really very angry.

It's a horrid silly name, he thought crossly, *and it's rude of people to call me that. They don't call that nice old gentleman with the beard 'Whiskers', do they? And they don't shout 'Nosy' at that boy with the big nose. I shan't answer them when they call me Whiskers!*

So he didn't – but it wasn't any good, for everyone

shouted 'Whiskers! Whiskers!' as soon as they saw Inky's wonderful whiskers.

Inky thought hard. 'I shall get rid of my whiskers,' he said to himself. 'Yes, I shall start a new fashion for cats. We won't have whiskers. After all, men shave every morning, and people think that is a good idea. I will shave my whiskers off, and then no one will call me Whiskers.'

He told his idea to wise old Shelly-Back the tortoise. Shelly-Back listened and pulled at the grass he was eating.

'It is best not to meddle with things you have been given,' he said. 'You will be sorry.'

'No, I shan't,' said Inky. 'My whiskers are no use to me that I can see – I shall shave them off!'

Well, he slipped into the bathroom at his home early the next morning and found the thing his master called a razor. In an instant Inky had shaved off his beautiful whiskers. They were gone. He was no longer a whiskery cat.

He looked at himself in the glass. He did look a bit strange – but at any rate no one would now shout 'Whiskers' after him. He slipped down the stairs and out into the garden. He jumped on the wall in the sun.

The milkman came by and looked at him. He did not shout 'Whiskers!' as he usually did. He stared in rather a puzzled way and said nothing at all. Then a young boy came by delivering papers, and he didn't shout 'Whiskers!' either.

Inky was pleased. At last he had got rid of his horrid name. He sat in the sun, purring, and soon his friends gathered round him. There was Tabby from next door, the white cat Snowball, Shelly-Back the tortoise, who looked up at him from the lawn, and the old dog Rover, who never chased cats.

'What's the matter with you this morning, Inky?' asked Snowball, puzzled. 'You look different.'

'His whiskers are gone,' said Tabby, startled. 'How strange!'

'How did you lose them?' asked Rover.

'I shaved them off,' Inky said proudly. 'I am starting a new fashion for cats. Grown-up men shave their whiskers off each day, don't they? Well, why should cats have whiskers? Don't you think I look much smarter now?'

Everyone stared at Inky, but nobody said a word. They all thought Inky looked dreadful without his whiskers.

'You'll soon see everyone following my fashion of no whiskers,' said Inky. 'It's much more comfortable. Whiskers always get in my way when I'm washing my face, but now I can wash it as smoothly as anything. Look!' He washed his face with his paw. Certainly it looked easier to do it without whiskers. But the older animals shook their heads.

'Whiskers must be some use or we wouldn't have them,' said Tabby.

'Well, what use are they?' said Inky.

But nobody was clever enough to think of anything to say in answer to that. One by one they slipped off to their homes to dinner, quite determined that they were not going to shave off their whiskers, whatever Inky did.

Now, that night Inky felt very hungry. He had been late for tea that afternoon and a stray dog had gone into his garden and eaten up the plate of fish and milk that his mistress had put out for him. Inky was annoyed.

Never mind, he thought to himself. *I'll go hunting tonight. I'll catch a few mice and perhaps a rat or two. I know a good place in the hedge at the bottom of the garden. I'll hide on one side of it and wait for the night animals to come out.*

So off he went when darkness came and crouched down on one side of the hedge. Soon he heard the pitter-pattering of little mice feet. Inky stiffened and kept quite still. In a moment he would squeeze through the hedge and pounce on those foolish mice.

He took a step forward. His paw was like velvet and made no noise. He pushed his head into a hole in the hedge – then his body – but alas for Inky! His body was too big for the hole, and the hedge creaked as he tried to get through. The mice heard the noise and shot off into their holes. Not one was left.

'Bother!' said Inky crossly. 'I'll wait again. I believe that old rat has a run here somewhere. I'd like to catch him!'

So he waited – and, sure enough, the big rat ran silently by the hedge. Inky heard him and began to creep towards him, but his fat body brushed against some leaves and the rat heard and fled.

Inky was astonished. Usually he could hunt marvellously without making a single sound. Why was it that his body seemed so clumsy tonight? Why did he brush against things and make rustling noises? It was most annoying.

And then suddenly he knew the reason why. Although he hadn't thought about it, his fine whiskers had always helped him to hunt. They had stretched out each side of his face, and were just about the width of his body. He had known that if he could get his head and whiskers through a hole without touching anything, his body would go through easily too without a sound.

It was my whiskers that helped my body to know if it could go easily and silently through the holes and between leaves, thought Inky in despair. *Of course! Why didn't I think of that before? They were just the right width for my body, and I knew quite well if I touched anything with my whiskers that my body would also touch it and make a noise – and so I would go another way!*

Inky was quite right. His whiskers had helped him in his hunting. Now he would not be able to hunt well, for he would never know if his body could squeeze through gaps and holes. He would always be making rustling, crackling noises with leaves and twigs. He would never catch anything. Poor Inky!

You can guess that Inky was always waiting for his mistress to put out his dinner after that – for he hardly ever caught a mouse or rat now. He grew much thinner, and he hid himself away, for he was ashamed to think that he had shaved off the things that had been so useful to him.

A new fashion indeed! thought Inky. *I was mad! If only I had my lovely whiskers again I wouldn't mind being called 'Whiskers' a hundred times a day. My life is spoilt. I shall never be able to hunt again.*

He was a sad and unhappy cat, ashamed to talk to anyone except wise old Shelly-Back the tortoise. One day he told Shelley-Back why he was unhappy. Shelly-Back looked at him closely and laughed.

'Go and sit up on the wall in the sun and see what happens,' he said to Inky. 'You'll find your troubles are not so big as you thought they were.'

In surprise Inky jumped up on the wall and sat there in the sun. The milkman came by with his cart. He looked up.

'Hello, Whiskers!' he shouted. 'Good old Whiskers!'

Inky nearly fell off the wall in astonishment. What? He was called Whiskers again even if he had shaved them off? But silly old Inky had quite forgotten something. What had he forgotten?

He had forgotten that whiskers grow again like hair. His whiskers had grown out fine and long and strong and white – and he had been so miserable that he hadn't even noticed. Silly old Whiskers!

He was happy when he found that he had them again. He sat and purred so loudly that Shelly-Back really thought there was an aeroplane flying somewhere near! It sounded just like it.

And now Inky can hunt again, and is the best mouser in the town. He has grown plump and handsome, and his whiskers are finer than ever. He loves to hear himself called Whiskers now. So if you see him up on the wall, black and shining, don't say 'Hello, Inky!' – shout 'Good old Whiskers!' and he'll purr like a kettle on the boil!

When the Donkey Sneezed

When the Donkey Sneezed

NEDDY THE donkey stood and looked at the cloudy sky. The sun had gone in a long time ago and the clouds were big and black.

Suddenly Neddy felt a sneeze coming. It was a great big sneeze, and he shut his eyes and opened his mouth.

'A-tish-ee-haw! A-tish-ee-haw!' he sneezed, very loudly indeed. That is the way that donkeys always sneeze, you know – a-tish-ee-haw! When the sneeze was finished Neddy opened his eyes again – and just at that very moment a most enormous wind blew up! My goodness me, it was a wind! The clouds shot across the sky in no time, the trees went wisha-wisha-wisha all together, as their hundreds of leaves brushed one against the other, and the flag on the church tower waved like mad.

'Well, look at that!' said Neddy the donkey, astonished and proud. 'That's what my sneeze has done – made this enormous wind! Would you believe it? I'm a very clever donkey, I am!'

Neddy didn't know that the wind had nothing at all to do with his sneeze. He really and truly thought that because he had sneezed such a big sneeze he had made the wind come all by himself. He was as pleased as could be. He straightened up his ears, flicked his tail round, and galloped over to where the ducks were waddling off the pond.

The wind had made such big waves there that they were afraid and were hurrying off the water. Neddy brayed loudly and spoke to them.

'Hee-haw! Do you know, I sneezed just now and made the big wind come that is blowing waves on your pond?'

'Quack!' said all the ducks together. 'Then we think you are very silly. Tell the wind to stop.'

But Neddy didn't stop to listen. He ran off to the hens, who were all huddling under the hedge out of the gale.

'Hee-haw! Do you know, I sneezed just now and made the big wind come that is blowing all your feathers up the wrong way?'

'Cluck!' the biggest brown hen said angrily. 'What a silly thing to do! Tell the wind to stop!'

Neddy hee-hawed loudly and laughed. He was very proud of having made the wind come because of his big sneeze.

'No,' he said, 'I shan't make the wind stop. I think it is a grand wind.'

'Cock-a-doodle-doo!' said a big cock crossly. 'You are stupid, Neddy. Look at my tail! It is almost blown off!'

But Neddy kicked up his heels and scampered away to the pigsty, where Mrs Sow and all her little pigs were crouching down in a corner, trying to keep out of the cold wind.

'Hee-haw! Do you know, I sneezed just now and made the big wind come that is blowing all the straw about in your sty?'

'Grunt!' said Mrs Sow, very annoyed. 'Well, tell it to stop, you silly donkey! Nobody likes a wind like this.'

'Oh, I shan't tell it to stop!' said Neddy. 'It is my wind, and a very nice wind too. Ho, ho, I'm a clever donkey, I am!'

Off he went again and galloped to the two brown horses that stood trying to shelter themselves under a tree. Their manes were blown upright in the wind and they shivered.

'Hee-haw! Do you know, I sneezed just now and made the big wind come that is blowing your manes about?' Neddy said proudly.

'What a silly thing to do on a cold day like this!' said the horses, neighing. 'Who wants a wind at this time of year? Make it stop at once!'

'Not I!' laughed Neddy, and trotted away to Tibbles, the farmyard cat, who was hiding under a bush, very much afraid of the stormy wind that was blowing her whiskers backwards.

'Hee-haw! Do you know, I sneezed just now and made the big wind come that is blowing your fur flat?' said Neddy proudly.

'Well, that's nothing to be proud of!' Tibbles said crossly. 'I was just drinking some milk out of my saucer on the kitchen step, and when the wind came it took hold of my saucer and tipped it up. Over went my milk and I lost my breakfast! Tell the wind to stop at once!'

'Not I!' laughed Neddy, pleased to think that so many things had happened because of his big sneeze. 'Ha, ha! What fun I am having!'

Well, all that day the wind blew, and what a nuisance it was! The flag blew right off the church tower, the big ash tree had a branch broken off, the pond was so rough that not even the biggest duck dared to swim on it, and it was really dangerous to cross the farmyard, because there were so many things blowing about in it. One little chick got quite lost in a big newspaper that suddenly blew over it, and its mother was very upset to hear it cheeping underneath. Altogether it was a dreadful day.

When teatime came all the farmyard animals met together and talked.

'Neddy the donkey must be made to stop this wind!' said one brown horse.

'We will tell him that if he doesn't sneeze again and stop it, we will pull his tail very hard indeed,' said the biggest duck.

'Let's go and find him,' said the cat. So off they went and found Neddy standing in the middle of the field, still feeling proud of his big wind, but shivering with cold.

'Neddy, you must stop this wind or we will all pull your tail hard,' said Mrs Sow, grunting.

'I don't know how to stop it,' said the donkey, rather frightened.

'Well, you started it with a sneeze, so I suppose you can stop it with a sneeze,' said a cock. 'We will all stand round you in a ring, and when we say "Go!" you must sneeze. Now, are you ready?'

All the animals and birds stood in a ring round the donkey, and the cock said, 'One, two, three – GO!'

Then they all listened for Neddy to sneeze – but he couldn't! You simply can't sneeze on purpose, can you? And no more could the donkey. He shut his eyes and opened his mouth ready for a good sneeze, but it wasn't a bit of good. It wouldn't come, and at last he shut his mouth and looked at the creatures round him.

'I can't sneeze, please,' he said in a very little voice.

'Nonsense!' said the cock. 'If you don't, we shall pull your tail!' But still Neddy couldn't sneeze, so one by one all the animals and birds pulled his tail – and you should have heard him bray! He was so upset!

While they were all doing this, the wind gradually dropped. Soon there was none at all, and the trees stood quite still and quiet. Nobody noticed that the wind had gone, and one by one all the animals and birds went home, leaving the poor donkey alone in the middle of his field.

It serves me right for being so proud! he thought. *But, dear me – look at this! The wind has gone! Now, what could have made it go? I didn't sneeze! Was it because I had my tail pulled that the wind stopped? Oh dear, if it was, I am afraid that all the animals will come and pull it again whenever they want the wind to stop. I couldn't bear that, so I will pack up my things and go far away where nobody knows about my sneeze.*

So he packed up the few things he had and galloped right away. Where he went to nobody knows, but I expect he is very careful about his sneezing, don't you?

The Banana Robber

The Banana Robber

JOHN, SHEILA and Mollie had a playroom up in the attic and they played there on rainy days. Mother let them have tea up there sometimes, and that was great fun. They carried up their mugs, plates, a jug of milk, three slices of cake and some apples or bananas. They were all very fond of fruit, and used to spend half their pocket money on it and store it in the playroom cupboard.

One day Uncle Jim gave John a shilling and he showed it to the others.

'I know what we'll do,' he said. 'I'll buy bananas with it, and we'll pretend we are cast on a lonely island where banana trees grow, and we'll eat them because there is nothing else and we might starve!'

'That would be a fine game to play,' said the two girls. 'Let's make some trees and tie the bananas on them.' So they borrowed poles from the potting shed and nailed leafy twigs on them for branches. They put them here and there in their playroom, and emptied some sand from their sand tray on the floor to make believe that it was the sandy shore of an island.

'The table upside down can be our boat,' said John. 'What fun we'll have! I'll be captain. Sheila, can you tie some bananas on this tree, and Mollie and I will do the others? There are fourteen bananas so we will be able to play this game two or three times before they are all eaten!'

Before they had finished getting things ready it was bedtime. The trees had their bananas on and looked fine. The table had the cloth for a sail and the floor was chalked with blue to make it look like the sea.

'We'll play the game tomorrow,' said John, and off they went to bed.

After tea the next day the three raced up to the playroom. There was the table, all ready to be a boat. There were the trees, all ready with their bananas. What fun!

'Now this table had better be a lifeboat, or a raft,' said John. 'Get in, you girls. We're escaping from a wrecked ship!'

They all got in. John swayed about as if the boat was rocking up and down on the sea. 'Hold on tight!' he shouted. 'I see land! Land ahoy! A lonely island! The tide is taking us there! Be ready to jump.'

The girls screamed and swayed about like John, pretending that the boat was rocked up and down. 'Now then!' cried John. 'We are near the beach. Jump! Jump for your lives!'

They all jumped out of the boat on to the sand. Sheila lay down as if she were tired out. John and

Mollie took off their overalls and squeezed them, pretending they were wet through.

'I'm so hungry!' moaned Sheila, sitting up. 'We shall starve here. There is nothing to eat.'

'Look! Look! Banana trees, with real bananas growing on them!' shouted John, jumping to his feet. 'Come and pick them.'

They went to the banana trees, and John gave a shout of surprise.

'I say! There are no bananas on my tree! Just look! Which of you girls has taken my bananas?'

'I haven't!' said Mollie.

'And I haven't!' said Sheila.

'Well, they're gone,' said John. 'And look – there is the peel on the floor. Oh, I say – it's too bad. Someone's been up and taken three of my bananas. I wonder who it can be.'

'Well, they're eaten,' said Mollie. 'You'll have to share our tree, John!'

So they gave John two bananas off their trees – but

the game was spoilt. It was so horrid to feel that someone had taken their bananas. It was such a mean trick.

'We'll play this game tomorrow,' said John. 'There are still some bananas left.'

Next evening after tea they raced upstairs again to their playroom, and the game began once more – but, would you believe it, before they had jumped out of the boat on to the sandy shore Mollie gave a shout. 'Look!' she said. 'There is some more peel on the floor. Someone has taken more of our bananas! Whoever can the robber be?'

'It's very strange,' said John, getting out of the boat and walking up to the peel thrown down on the floor. 'It's not any of us, that's certain, for we'd tell each other if it were. And it can't be anyone in the house, or we'd see them going up here!'

'Shall we hide behind the cupboard door and see if we can find out who the robber is?' cried Mollie. 'Do let's!'

'All right,' said John. 'Come on. Let's hide now. The robber might come any time.'

So, very quietly, they crouched behind the big cupboard door and peeped through the crack to watch who the robber might be. They waited a long time, but nobody came. John watched the door, and he kept thinking it was opening little by little, but it wasn't.

'I'm getting tired of this,' whispered Mollie. 'Let's go out now and play, John, shall we?'

'Perhaps we'd better,' said John. 'The banana robber isn't coming this evening!'

But even as he spoke the three children heard a noise. They held their breaths and looked at the door. But nothing came round it. They heard the noise again – a little scraping sound – and it came from the window, not the door! The children peered through the crack. Who could it be at the window?

A strange little face looked in – a little brown face with bright dark eyes. Then in at the window came – what do you think? Yes, a small monkey! He jumped in and ran to the trees stuck up here and there on the floor. He ran up one and pulled a banana down. He slid down to the floor with a little happy chattering sound. He peeled the banana and bit off a piece of the yellow fruit inside. Then he threw down the peel and went up the tree again!

'So that's the banana robber!' said John, and he ran out of the cupboard. 'Come on, you girls – this is a real desert island now with monkeys and everything! Hurrah!'

The monkey looked up in surprise. He seemed pleased to see John. He made a little chattering noise again and suddenly jumped right into John's arms! The little boy was startled, but very pleased to find the small monkey so friendly. He hugged him, and the two girls came up and stroked him.

'Let's take him downstairs and show Mummy,' said John. So down they went. Mummy was astonished.

'Why, he must be the monkey that Mrs Bailey lost last week!' she said. 'He escaped and went up on the roof of her house, and then she lost sight of him. He must have lived up on the roofs for a few days – and, seeing the bananas on your make-believe trees, he crept in to get them for food. You'd better take him back.'

So the children took him back to Mrs Bailey, and when she heard that he had stolen their bananas what do you think she did? She gave them a shilling to make up for the stolen bananas, and another shilling for bringing back the monkey.

'Now we can buy bananas, apples and oranges!' said John joyfully. And off they went to the greengrocer's. Weren't they lucky?

The Beautiful Big Bone

The Beautiful Big Bone

ONCE UPON a time Bundle the spaniel had a beautiful big bone. It had two nobbly ends and a long thick middle, and it smelt lovely.

Bundle was very proud of his bone. He didn't show it to Cosy the cat because he was afraid she might gnaw one of the ends off. Bundle spent an awfully long time gnawing on the bone, and when he was tired of it he hid it, so that when he wanted another chew at it he would know where to find it.

I'll hide it in the cabbage bed, Bundle thought. *No one goes there now. I think it will be a very good place.*

So he dug away the earth and hid it there. Cosy

saw him and wondered what he could be doing. The next day Bundle dug up his bone again and had another good chew at it. Then he carried it off in his mouth to bury it once more.

'Are you going to put that in the cabbage bed again?' asked Cosy, meeting him round the corner.

Bundle growled at her. 'You mind your own business!' he said.

Bundle trotted off, thinking hard. What a nuisance! Now Cosy knew exactly where he had decided to hide his bone.

Never mind! thought Bundle. *I'll hide it somewhere else – somewhere that Cosy will never guess! I'll hide it in the rubbish heap!*

So he went to the rubbish heap at the bottom of the garden and dug in the rubbish there to hide his bone.

Cosy watched him from under a bush. *I suppose Bundle doesn't want his bone any more, as he's putting it on the rubbish heap*, thought Cosy. *Well, I'll have a lick at it when he's gone.*

So, when Bundle had gone indoors to snooze by the fire Cosy scampered over to the rubbish heap. She soon found the beautiful big bone and she dragged it out. She took it into a quiet corner where she began to lick it.

Her tongue was very rough and she managed to scrape off a few bits of meat. Then she decided it would be lovely to gnaw the bone, but her teeth were simply not strong enough.

'Woof!' said a voice in her ear suddenly, and made her jump high into the air. 'Lend me that bone, Cosy!'

It was Shadow, the big sheepdog from the farm. He was a gentle fellow, and Cosy was not afraid of him.

'All right,' she said. 'You can have it, because I'm sure Bundle doesn't want it any more. He put it on the rubbish heap.'

'What a stupid dog!' said Shadow, and picked up the bone to carry it away. He took it to the farmyard, went into his kennel with it, and lay there, licking and gnawing very happily.

Now, when Bundle went to the rubbish heap to his great surprise he found no bone there. He sat down and wailed miserably. It wasn't long before Cosy heard him.

'Whatever can the matter be?' she said.

'My beautiful bone's gone!' cried Bundle, and he wailed again.

'It's all right. Shadow has got it,' said Cosy, and was just going to explain that she had lent it to him when Bundle tore off down the garden, out of the gate and into the lane that led to the farm, before Cosy could say another word to him.

Bundle arrived at the farm. He saw Shadow gnawing his beautiful big bone. He went as near as he dared and spoke to Shadow.

'Give me that bone. It's mine.'

'Ask for it politely,' said Shadow, giving a crunch that sounded very loud to Bundle.

'Don't bite it in half, don't!' wailed poor Bundle. 'It's my bone! Give it to me at once, Shadow, you bad dog!'

'Not if you talk like that,' said Shadow, licking the bone well.

'Well, what do you want for that bone?' said Bundle at last, thinking that if he didn't get the bone quickly, there wouldn't be any to get.

'I wouldn't mind a nice drink of milk,' said Shadow. 'I feel very thirsty. You get me a jug of milk and I'll give you the bone.'

Bundle ran off to Buttercup the cow. 'Could you give me some milk?' he said.

Buttercup looked at him and chewed hard. 'I might, if you'll go and ask Neddy the donkey in the next field if he'll let me have one of his carrots,' said Buttercup. 'I just feel somehow I'd like to taste a carrot today.'

'Oh, tails and whiskers – Neddy's right at the end of the next field!' said poor Bundle. 'By the time I get to him and back, and get some milk and take it to Shadow, my bone will have been eaten!'

But he raced across the field, squeezed under the

gate and ran to Neddy, who was crunching up a few carrots the farmer's wife had given him.

'Neddy, will you give me a carrot for Buttercup the cow?' asked Bundle, panting.

'Well, you'll have to give me something in return,' said Neddy. 'You go and get me a fine thistle plant to eat.'

'What? Do you eat thistles?' said Bundle, surprised. 'Aren't they very prickly?'

'Yes. They're delicious,' said Neddy. 'Go and get me some. Do you see Bleater the goat over there on the common? Well, there are some fine thistles near him. He will show you them.'

Off went poor Bundle again, and came to Bleater, who put down his head and danced round and round Bundle as if he was going to butt him.

'No, don't do that, Bleater. I've only come for some thistles,' said Bundle. 'Tails and whiskers, aren't they prickly? I can't possibly bite them and take them to Neddy. I should make my mouth bleed.'

'Well, I'll pick them for you if you like,' said Bleater at once. 'My mouth is hard. I don't mind anything. But what will you give me if I do?'

'Oh dear, everyone wants something today,' said Bundle. 'What do you want, Bleater?'

'Well, do you see that hole in the hedge there?' said Bleater. 'There's a hen sitting there on eggs she has laid. I've always wanted to eat an egg, Bundle. You go and get one for me. My rope won't reach to that gap in the hedge.'

So Bundle ran off to the gap and nosed his way to the hen. She pecked him and he yelped.

'What do you want?' she said.

'An egg for Bleater, please,' said Bundle. The hen gave an angry cluck.

'An egg! What next? For nothing, I suppose?'

'Well, what do you want for it?' said Bundle. The hen put her head on one side and thought hard for a moment.

'One of the eggs I'm sitting on is addled,' she said.

'I don't mind Bleater having that one, and I dare say a goat would rather eat a bad egg than a good one. You go and get me some corn, Bundle, and then I'll give you the egg.'

Bundle ran off to the corn bin. He knew where it was. But sitting beside it was Cosy!

'Get away, Cosy, I want some corn,' said Bundle.

'Be quiet, Bundle!' said Cosy. 'I'm watching for the mouse that comes to this bin. You'll frighten it away if you bark like that. Besides, you know very well you don't eat corn!'

'I want it for the hen,' Bundle said crossly. 'Get away, Cosy, and let me open the bin.'

'Now listen to me, Bundle,' said Cosy. 'Don't bother about corn for the hen. You go off home and look in your dish. I've put something there for you!'

'Yes, a fishbone you can't swallow, I suppose!' said Bundle. 'Now move away, Cosy, and let me get this corn.'

'Well, I'll move away if you let me have half your dinner tonight,' said Cosy.

Bundle groaned. Everybody wanted something. 'All right,' he said. 'You can share my dinner, but do let me get the corn.'

Cosy moved away. Bundle lifted up the lid and put his nose in. He got a mouthful of corn and ran off to the hen with it.

He scattered it by her and she pecked it up, clucking loudly. 'Now you can have the egg,' she said. 'The one on the outside, just there.'

Bundle picked it up in his mouth and ran off to Bleater the goat with the egg. Bleater was delighted. He pulled up a whole thistle for Bundle, and then ate the egg. It smelt horrible to Bundle, but Bleater thought it was delicious.

Bundle dragged the thistle along by its root. It was the only part of it that wasn't too prickly to hold. He came at last to Neddy the donkey.

'Ah,' said Neddy, 'just in time! I was going to eat

my last carrot, but now you can have it in exchange for this fine thistle.'

He gave Bundle a carrot, and then began to crunch up the thistle. Bundle thought it was marvellous not to bother about eating sharp prickles like that. He ran off with the carrot.

Buttercup the cow was waiting. Bundle gave her the carrot and she nibbled at it daintily. 'I have no teeth in my top jaw, so it's not as easy to eat a carrot as it is to pull grass,' she said. 'Still, it's very tasty. There is some milk in a small pail for you over there, Bundle. Can you pick up the handle in your mouth and take it along like that?'

Bundle just managed to, though he spilt a little of the milk on the way. Still, there was plenty left in the pail when he reached Shadow the sheepdog, who was still lying in his kennel.

'Woof!' said Shadow, and drank up the milk at once. 'Most delicious! Thank you!'

'Where's my beautiful big bone?' said Bundle,

looking around in alarm. 'Oh, Shadow – you haven't eaten it, have you?'

'No,' said Shadow. 'I gave it back to Cosy. She came and fetched it.'

'Well!' said Bundle, and tore off to find Cosy, quite determined to chase her all around the garden and back again if she had taken his bone.

'Cosy! How dare you take my bone from Shadow!' wuffed Bundle, out of breath.

'Well, Bundle, you were so upset about it,' said Cosy. 'So I went and told him it was yours, and he gave it back to me for you. It's in your dish. I put it there myself. I don't know why you wanted to go rushing around the garden getting corn for hens and things like that all the afternoon!'

'Now, look here, Cosy!' said Bundle fiercely. 'Shadow said he'd give me back my bone if I gave him some milk from Buttercup the cow. And she said she'd give me milk if I got a carrot from Neddy for her. And he said he'd give me a carrot if I got him a thistle.

And Bleater the goat said he'd give me the thistle if I got him a hen's egg to eat. And the hen said she'd give me an egg if I got her some corn. And *you* said you'd let me have the corn if I gave you half my dinner tonight. And all the time I was rushing about getting presents for everybody my big beautiful bone was sitting in my dish waiting for me!'

Cosy began to laugh. Bundle stared crossly at her. Then he looked so fierce she began to feel rather alarmed.

'I'm going to chase you all around the garden and then bite the hairs off the end of your tail!' said Bundle.

'Now, Bundle, listen – while you do that someone may come along and take your bone out of its dish!' said Cosy, edging away. 'Do be sensible, and go and get it while it's safe!'

So poor Bundle ran off to get his bone. He lay in a corner and chewed it. Then he began to laugh. Yes, it was funny the way he had rushed all over the place findings things for people, so that he could get back his bone – and all the time it was waiting for him in his dish!

'You can share my dinner with me if you like!' he called out to Cosy. 'Why don't we tell Mistress what I've done this afternoon, and let me make it into a story, shall we?'

So he did – and here it is!

Good Old Shelly-Back!

Good Old Shelly-Back!

SHELLY-BACK WAS a tortoise. He was a very big one too, and Mary and Jack were proud of him. They always put him to bed in a box of earth each autumn, so that he might sleep soundly in the cold potting shed. Mary had made him a little blanket with his name on it – 'Shelly-Back' – and she carefully covered him up with it.

In the spring he always woke up and crawled around his box. Then the children took him out and put him in the garden. How he did enjoy the warm spring sunshine! He would poke out his little head and look up at the sun in delight.

Mary used to borrow the polish from Cook and take a duster and give Shelly-Back's great shell a good polish, so that it shone beautifully. He liked the two children and would let him tickle him under the chin without going back into his shell.

And then one day Daddy was dreadfully cross with Shelly-Back.

'That tortoise of yours has got on to the beds and eaten all my young delphinium plants!' said Daddy angrily. 'It's too bad.'

'But, Daddy, they will grow again,' said Mary.

'Grow again!' said Daddy. 'Yes, I dare say they will – but it will take a long time.'

Then one day Daddy was angrier still.

'Shelly-Back has eaten half my pansy plants!' he said. 'Can't you keep him off the beds, you children? What's the good of my spending money and time on the garden if your stupid tortoise behaves like that? You had better give him away.'

'Oh, no, Daddy!' cried Jack. 'He's our only pet.

We are very fond of him. We will try to watch and see that he doesn't get on the beds.'

They did try – but one day they went out to tea, and when they came back they found Daddy very cross indeed again. Shelly-Back had eaten his new young lettuces!

'Now look here, children,' said Daddy, 'I'm very, very sorry – but I'm afraid the tortoise will have to go. I'm not going to have him spoiling the garden like this. We only have a small garden and every inch is precious. Shelly-Back is doing a lot of damage.'

Mary and Jack were unhappy. They went out into the garden and looked at the tortoise. He stared up at them and moved his funny little head from side to side.

'He's a nice tortoise,' said Jack. 'I don't want to give him away. We have had him for three years now. He will grow bigger and bigger and be a monster tortoise, I should think, if only Daddy would let us keep him.'

Mary bent down to tickle the tortoise under the

chin. Then she gave a cry and pointed to the back of his shell.

'Look, Jack!' she said. 'He has a little hole in his shell. Suppose we thread it with string – a very long piece – and tie the other end to a post, so that he can have a good long walk around the lawn, but can't get on to Daddy's beds. Perhaps that will be all right!'

So they threaded the little hole with string and tied the other end to a post. Shelly-Back was quite happy. He walked all round the lawn, but he couldn't get on to the beds because his string wouldn't let him. Jack gave him fresh greens to eat each day, so he was very happy.

But Daddy wasn't. He kept saying that the tortoise was still eating his lettuces. 'Two or three go every day,' he grumbled. 'It must be that tortoise. He will have to go, children. I know you say he is safely on a string – but he must get loose, because every morning when I go to look at my lettuces there are a few gone.'

Mary and Jack didn't know what to do. They

tied Shelly-Back up more tightly than ever, so that he couldn't possibly get loose – but the very next morning Daddy said that two more of his best lettuces had disappeared.

'I have told old Mr Brown he can have the tortoise,' Daddy said at breakfast. 'He doesn't grow anything except grass in his garden so Shelly-Back can't do much damage there. I will take him tomorrow.'

Poor Mary and Jack! They could have cried with disappointment, but it wasn't a bit of good. Daddy wouldn't change his mind. He went off to the office as usual, and Mary and Jack went to school.

Now, it happened that the next morning Daddy thought he would get up early and do a bit of gardening. So at six o'clock he got up and dressed. He stood at the window, fastening his collar, when he saw something that made him stare. It was a small boy creeping in at the back gate! Daddy wondered what he was doing, so early in the morning. Then he suddenly guessed!

He's after my lettuces! thought Daddy. *He's the little thief! I'll soon catch him and give him a good telling off!*

He tore downstairs, waking up Mary and Jack, who ran to the window to see what could be happening. Daddy was going out of the garden door to catch the little boy. But the small thief saw him and, his hands full of lettuces, he turned to run.

'Daddy won't catch him now,' said Jack in excitement. 'Look, it's Billy, that naughty little boy who always calls out rude things to people! Oh, look, he's dodged Daddy, and he's running over the lawn to the front gate. He'll get away now.'

But he didn't get away! What do you think happened? Why, the boy ran across the lawn and didn't see the string that tied up Shelly-Back the tortoise. His foot caught in it and over he went, bump! Before he could pick himself up, Daddy had caught him and was giving him a good telling off. He made him promise never to steal lettuces again, and then sent him off, saying that he would tell his father the very next time he heard of him doing anything wrong.

And that morning, at breakfast, Daddy said that he was not going to take old Shelly-Back to Mr Brown.

'He wasn't the thief after all,' he said.

'But he caught the thief for you, Daddy!' laughed Jack. 'We saw him!'

'He certainly did!' said Daddy. 'Well, you can keep him. He was most useful to me this morning, and I am grateful to him because he has certainly saved the rest of my lettuces!'

So old Shelly-Back still lives with Mary and Jack. He is very big now, and his back shines as brightly as ever. If you go to tea with Mary and Jack, he will let you tickle him under his chin – but not if it's wintertime, for he will be fast asleep in his box then!

Hoo-Hoo's Party

Hoo-Hoo's Party

HOO-HOO THE owl was very hungry. He hadn't caught a mouse or a rabbit for a week, though he had tried hard every night. Whatever should he do?

He sat in his hollow tree and thought hard. Then a wonderful idea came to him.

'I will give a party,' he said to himself. 'I will ask Whiskers the mouse, Tailer the rat, Soft-Ears the rabbit, Singer the nightingale, Mowdie the mole and Frisky the squirrel. Ha, ha, hoo, hoo!'

So he sent out his invitations, and this is what the cards said:

Hoo-Hoo the owl

invites

Whiskers the mouse

to a party

on the next full moon

night in the

hollow tree.

He sent the cards, each with the name of the person written on it, to Whiskers, Tailer, Soft-Ears, Singer, Mowdie and Frisky. Then he waited for the answers.

Whiskers the mouse was delighted. He had never been to a party in his life. So he accepted gratefully.

Tailer the rat was always hungry, and the thought of a party made him joyful. He thought that he would get there early and eat a lot. So he accepted too.

Soft-Ears the rabbit read his invitation over and over again very proudly. He had only once been to a party, and it had been so lovely that he had always longed to go to another. So he accepted the invitation too, and wrote a neat little answer.

Singer the nightingale felt quite certain that she had been invited because of her lovely voice.

I expect they will ask me to sing, she thought. *That will be nice, for they will all praise my beautiful voice.* So she accepted too, and sent her answer along that same day.

Mowdie the mole had been to hundreds and hundreds of parties, and he felt certain that he had another one on the same night. But when he looked in his notebook to see, he found that he hadn't. So he decided that he would go, and he scribbled an answer at once.

Frisky the squirrel read Hoo-Hoo's card carefully. Then he read it again. Then he read it for a third time.

He didn't like Hoo-Hoo, and he felt quite certain that Hoo-Hoo didn't like him.

Why then had he been asked to Hoo-Hoo's party?

'There is something funny about this,' said Frisky,

who was very wise for his age. 'I wonder who else has been asked.'

So he went around to the other animals to find out, and when he heard that Whiskers the mouse, Tailer the rat, Mowdie the mole, Soft-Ears the rabbit and Singer the nightingale had been asked he sat and thought hard again.

At last he took his fountain pen and wrote to say that he would go.

Then he went round to all the others and said that he would call for them on the party night, and would they please be ready before the moon was up.

'But why?' they asked. 'Hoo-Hoo doesn't want us till the moon is shining.'

'Never mind,' said Frisky. 'You do as I tell you, and you will be glad afterwards.'

So on the party night everyone was ready before the moon was up. The woods were all in darkness, and Frisky went quietly round to Whiskers, Tailer, Soft-Ears, Singer and Mowdie.

'We will all go to the hollow tree and peep inside it to see what Hoo-Hoo the owl has got for the party,' said Frisky. 'But we won't go by the front way. I know a little hole at the back and we will peep in there, so that Hoo-Hoo won't see us.'

So they all set off together, and they didn't make a scrap of noise. Soon they came to the hollow tree, and Frisky led them round to the little hole at the back and they all peeped through.

Just then the moon came up, and the little guests could see inside quite plainly.

And to their very great astonishment there was nothing to eat at all! Not a single thing! There was a big dish, quite empty, and five empty plates.

'Good gracious!' whispered Mowdie. 'This is a funny sort of party!'

'Where are all the cakes and jellies and things?'

'Shh!' said Frisky. 'Can't you hear someone coming?'

The animals all listened and looked. And whatever do you think they saw?

Why, Hoo-Hoo the owl coming into the hollow tree with four of his friends, all owls like himself!

'Sit down,' he said. 'Our dinner will be here soon. We have only got to wait! I do hope you'll enjoy the party.'

The owls all sat down and waited. The little creatures outside hardly dared to breathe. They suddenly knew what the dinner was! It was themselves!

Then one by one they crept away to their homes. Whiskers went to his hole, Tailer went to his. Soft-Ears scampered to his burrow, and Singer flew to her bush. Mowdie went to his nest, and only Frisky was left.

He wasn't afraid of Hoo-Hoo and he kept his eye to the hole in the tree to see what would happen. The owls waited and waited and waited, but of course their dinner didn't come. It had all gone home long ago!

The four owls flew at Hoo-Hoo in a rage and pecked him hard till he hooted in fright. Then they flew out of the hollow tree in a temper and left Hoo-Hoo by himself.

Then Frisky called out cheekily, 'how did your party go, Hoo-Hoo? Did you have a nice time?'

He didn't wait for Hoo-Hoo to answer, not he! He fled up to the top of the tree and hid there in safety, chuckling to himself to think how angry the owl would be. So he was – and he never gave a party again in all his life!

Tinker-Dog and Prince

Tinker-Dog and Prince

TINKER-DOG LIVED with his master in a little tumbledown cottage at the end of Tiptop Village. He wasn't a terrier, and he wasn't a collie, and he wasn't an Alsatian. I couldn't tell you what he was – he just wasn't anything but a plain dog. But his master loved him and called him a fine fellow.

Prince was a beautiful Alsatian dog, so like a grand wolf that you could hardly tell he wasn't. He was worth a lot of money, and he was as proud as could be. He walked along the road as if it belonged to him, and if he met Tinker-Dog he growled at him angrily.

'Growl away, Prince High and Mighty!' Tinker

barked back. 'I can race you any day, though you run like the wind! My legs are as good as yours!'

'Common little dog!' said Prince in his deep growly voice. 'Keep out of my way. I am a prize dog. I win prizes at shows. You wouldn't win a prize at all – except for the ugliest, commonest dog in the show. Woooooof!'

Tinker-Dog ran home. He was sometimes a bit sad because he knew quite well he was a common little dog, and would certainly never win a prize at any show. He didn't want a prize for himself – but it would be so nice to win a prize for his master, whom he loved very much!

Now, one day Prince and Tinker met by the river. 'Woooooof!' said Prince, snarling at Tinker-Dog. 'Why don't you keep out of my way? I don't like your looks. I don't like your smell. I don't like your—'

'I don't like your manners!' said Tinker, and he actually bit the end of Prince's tail! What would have happened next I don't know – but, just at that moment, a little boy who was playing by the river suddenly gave a scream and fell right into the water!

'Help! Help!' shouted the other children. Prince stared at the water. Tinker-Dog stared too and barked to Prince: 'You are a big strong dog. Jump in and pull the little boy out!'

But Prince ran away! It was Tinker-Dog who jumped into the cold water and swam bravely to the little boy. He caught hold of the child's coat and then turned back to the bank. How heavy the little boy was! Tinker-Dog puffed and panted, but he didn't let go! He struggled on and on.

'Look at that good little dog!' suddenly cried a man's voice. 'He's got the child safely! Come on – let's help him!'

But Tinker needed no help. Just at that moment he reached the bank, and the little boy, spluttering and choking, climbed out, pulled by the other children.

'Brave dog! Good dog!' cried all the watching people, for there was now quite a crowd by the river.

'Who is he? Why, he is the little dog belonging to Mr Brown!'

Tinker-Dog didn't know what all the fuss was about. He shook himself well and ran off home.

'Brave dog! Good dog!' everyone shouted after him. And then someone said, 'I saw that great big Alsatian dog called Prince run away! He didn't rescue Tommy! He was a coward – he ran away and left the job to a dog three times as small as himself! Tinker-Dog deserves a medal!'

Soon the news about Tinker-Dog was all around the town! A newspaper man came to see Tinker-Dog's master and took Tinker's photograph! It was in the paper next morning and underneath Tinker's picture it said:

'The finest dog in our town, Tinker-Dog, who saved little Tommy from the river! What shall we give him for a reward?'

Now, the next week there was a dog show in the town, and, of course, Prince was going, for he hoped to win the best prizes. And, do you know, a man came to Tinker-Dog's master and asked him to take Tinker too.

'He won't win a prize for being a beautiful dog,' he said, 'but the dog show people want to give him a medal and a fine red collar because he is the bravest dog they know. Little Tommy is to give it to him!'

So Tinker-Dog, much to his surprise, was taken to the show, nicely washed and brushed. Prince went too – and when he saw Tinker-Dog he laughed and said, 'Fancy you turning up at my show, Tinker! Coming to see me take all the prizes?'

'Hello, funny-face!' said Tinker-Dog, and ran along beside his master.

Prince did win a prize – but, oh dear, what do you suppose he felt like, when, at the end of the show, he saw the chief judge go up on to the platform and call for Tinker-Dog?

'Now we come to the most important dog in the town!' said the judge, patting Tinker, who wagged his tail and looked most surprised. 'This is Tinker-Dog, who saved little Tommy from drowning last week. Prince, the big, prize-winning Alsatian, was by the river too – but he ran away! It was little Tinker-Dog that jumped into the water! Three cheers for Tinker-Dog!'

'Hip hip hip hurrah!' shouted everyone. And then up to the platform walked little Tommy, carrying a fine red collar with a silver medal hanging from it!

He put the collar round Tinker's neck. How the medal shone and glittered when Tinker wagged his stumpy tail! He was the happiest dog in the world. His master was sitting nearby, looking so pleased and proud of his dog. Tinker wuffed to him. 'I've won a prize for you, master! I may be a common little dog, but I've done something after all!'

Everyone went home talking of Tinker-Dog. Prince went home too, his tail drooping. What did it matter winning a prize for being splendid and beautiful to look at? Nobody looked at him – they all wanted to see Tinker, that common little dog! Prince sat by the fire and thought and thought.

It isn't good looks that matter after all, or even good manners! he thought to himself. *It is good deeds. I must tell Tinker when I see him.*

So the next time he saw Tinker he ran over to him. 'Tinker-Dog, I may be a grand-looking dog, but you are a better dog than I am,' he said. 'I'd like to be friends with you, if you'll let me.'

'Wuff-wuff! Of course,' said Tinker. 'Pleased to go for a walk with you any day, Prince!'

And now the two are always seen together, and perhaps one day Prince will be able to show that he can be as brave as Tinker. What do you think?

Boo! Boo! Boo!

Boo! Boo! Boo!

HARRY WAS to go and stay with his aunt and uncle at Tall-Trees Farm. His mother took him there, and Uncle Jim and Aunt Nell looked at the small quiet boy.

'Harry's so shy,' said his mother. 'He's timid too – jumps at the least noise. I do hope you will see that the dogs don't jump up at him, because if they do he'll be terribly frightened.'

'It would be easier to train Harry not to be timid than to teach dogs not to come jumping around us,' said Uncle Jim. 'A farm's no place to come if you're going to scream whenever a dog comes near!'

'Oh dear! I do hope you will be gentle with Harry,' said his mother. 'He really is so shy. Goodbye, Harry. Enjoy yourself, and do what you are told.'

Harry was scared of going to the farm. He was afraid of cows and sheep, he thought the horses were far too big, and he couldn't bear the dogs that came bounding around. Uncle Jim hadn't much patience with him, but Aunt Nell was sorry for the little boy and tried not to let him be frightened.

But, really, Harry was too silly for words! When a hen came clucking around his feet he screamed for his aunt. 'Aunt Nell! Aunt Nell! This hen's going to attack me! She's pecked at me!'

Aunt Nell came running at once – but when she saw that it was only a hen Harry was frightened of she laughed. 'Oh, Harry! How can you be so silly? Look, the hen has seen your shoelace is undone, and it looks like a worm to her. That's what she's pecking at.'

Now, one day Harry left the gate of his aunt's garden open, and when the geese in the field beyond wandered near it, one of them walked right in at the gate.

The goose saw the nice green rows of lettuces in Aunt Nell's garden, and went to peck at them. Peck, peck, peck! Those lettuces soon disappeared.

Harry was just by the gate when the goose came in. It was a big bird with a very long neck, and Harry was terrified to see it come walking in at the gate. He saw it go to his aunt's lettuces and eat them. He crouched under a bush, hoping that the goose would not see him. He was so afraid of it that he hardly dared to breathe.

Soon his uncle came by and saw the goose. In a rage he ran at it, and soon that goose was flying for its life to the other end of the field. Then Uncle Jim saw Harry hiding under the bush. He was most astonished.

'What are you doing there? Didn't you see that goose eating your aunt's lettuces? Why didn't you chase it away?'

Harry crawled out from under the bush. 'Oh, Uncle, it frightened me. It looked so big and fierce. I wouldn't have dared to chase it.'

His uncle looked very angry. 'Now, see here!' he said with a frown. 'I never thought I'd meet a boy who couldn't say boo to a goose. Never! I'm ashamed of you. Something has got to be done about this. Hiding from a goose, indeed! Not even daring to say boo. Little coward. You're not shy; you're cowardly, Harry.'

Harry began to cry, so you can see what a silly he was. 'Now stop that,' said his uncle. 'I'm not your mother or your aunt, ready to rush to you with a handkerchief – I'm your uncle, and I'm going to teach you a lesson.'

'Oh, no, no,' wept Harry.

'Oh, yes, yes,' said Uncle Jim. 'Now you'll see what I'm going to do. You're to stand here – just by the gate. Come along.'

Harry went and stood by the gate. Uncle Jim

opened it. 'Now I'm going to chase a goose into the garden,' he said, 'and you are to get it out. Understand?'

'But it won't go out for me,' wept Harry.

'You say boo to it, and try,' said Uncle Jim. 'How old are you – eight years, or eight months? Good gracious me, what a baby you are! Now just you stand there and say boo!'

So, very frightened, Harry stood by the gate and watched his uncle chase a goose towards him. It came flapping in at the gate. Harry was so terrified that he could hardly open his mouth. But at last he did.

'Boo!' he said. It was rather a feeble boo, but at least it was a boo.

The goose stared at him, frightened, but it didn't go away. 'Boo!' said Harry again, seeing his uncle coming along.

The goose gave a frightened cackle and shot out of the gate at once. Harry was most surprised, and very relieved. He stopped crying.

'Here comes another!' cried his uncle, and sent in a second goose, which was hissing fiercely.

'Boo,' said Harry, and the goose shot out of the gate just as the other had done.

'Now this one!' called his uncle. 'Oh, there are two coming!'

And two enormous cackling geese came in at the gate, and seemed as if they were going to walk straight over to Harry.

'BOO!' he yelled, half frightened. And the geese fled away on their big feet as fast as they could. Harry was astonished and very pleased indeed. Gracious! The geese were really much more scared of him than he was of them!

'Now these hens!' called his uncle, and Harry saw a little flock of hens coming along, attracted by the noise. They walked in at the gate, clucking at each other. They knew quite well they shouldn't go into the garden.

'Shoo!' said Harry, and the hens shooed away at once.

'Aha!' said Uncle Jim, coming up. 'So you can say boo to a goose and shoo to a hen. You're growing up! See that I don't have to teach you lessons like this again, or I shall be so ashamed of you that I shall send you home.'

Harry thought about the geese and the hens that night. *Fancy me being scared of them when they are so scared of me*, he thought. *No wonder Uncle Jim thought I was a coward. All the same, I am a coward really. I can say boo to a goose and shoo to a hen now, but I don't think I could say: 'Come to heel, sir!' to Uncle Jim's big dog!*

Still, he tried it the next day when Rover was jumping about around him, splashing him with water from the puddles in the farmyard. Although he was frightened of the big dog, Harry spoke to him sternly in the kind of voice he had heard his uncle use.

'Come to heel, sir! How dare you! Come to heel!'

And Rover put down his tail, and came quietly over to Harry, standing with his nose almost touching the little boy's ankle.

'It's marvellous,' said Harry, patting Rover to make him put up his tail again. 'I feel quite different!'

Now, two days later, somebody left the garden gate open again, and this time seven cows wandered in! They went straight to the rows of peas that Aunt Nell had grown and began to munch them, pods and all.

Harry saw them from the window, and screamed, 'Aunt Nell! Quick, the cows are in the garden!'

But Aunt Nell was out, and Uncle Jim was over in the big barn a good distance away. Only Harry was there. He watched a cow with long, sharp-looking horns pull down half a row of peas and begin to munch happily. The little boy knew how proud his aunt was of her peas, and he was upset. But how could he deal with cows? They were not geese or hens that could be booed or shooed, or dogs to be told to come to heel. They were big, heavy, lumbering creatures, with horns that could hurt if they were stuck into anyone.

'I'm scared,' said Harry, beginning to tremble.

'I really am frightened of cows. I daren't go out into the garden. Yes, I'm a coward all right, even though I thought I wasn't any more.'

The cows started on some beans. Oh dear, those were for next Sunday's dinner! Harry suddenly forgot that he was a coward and ran out.

'Boo!' he yelled. The cows lifted their heads and stared at him, but they didn't take more notice than that. They went on munching and munching.

'Shoo!' yelled Harry, but they didn't take any notice of that either.

'Well, come to heel then, you bad creatures!' shouted Harry, wondering if they would, and hoping that they wouldn't. They didn't, of course. They just went on munching.

What am I to do? thought Harry. Then he saw the nearest cow looking at him, and he thought she was staring at him very scornfully, thinking, *Ha! What a little coward!*

'I'm not then!' shouted Harry, and he darted

indoors to the hall. He found his uncle's walking stick and ran out again. He brandished it at the cows.

'Bad cows! Get out! Go away! See this stick, it's for cows who won't go when they're told!'

The cows didn't like the look of the stick. The one nearest to Harry lumbered away to the gate. Harry yelled again, and actually ran at a big red and white cow. She put down her head and he stopped, not liking the look of her horns. She mooed and Harry almost jumped out of his skin. He turned to run away, but managed to stop himself.

'Go away, I tell you!' he shouted, and waved his stick again.

And then, to his great relief and delight, the big cows all turned and lumbered out of the gate!

When the last one had gone Harry shut the gate. He was shaking at the knees, but he was very pleased with himself. Then he heard a voice from behind him, and he jumped.

'Well, well, well! So he's not a coward after all! He

can chase out big cows with horns, as well as boo at geese and shoo hens away!'

It was Uncle Jim. Harry turned and gave a rather trembly smile.

'They went out all right, didn't they? But all the same I was scared, Uncle. I'm still a coward at heart.'

'If you can be brave when you are feeling scared, that's better still,' said Uncle Jim. 'That's the stuff that heroes are made of, Harry. I shan't call you a coward any more. You're not!'

Harry was very happy at the farm after that. He wasn't scared of anything at all, not even of the big bull who bellowed at him.

It was a good thing his uncle taught him to say boo to a goose, wasn't it?

It's Nice to Have a Friend

It's Nice to Have a Friend

TIBS WAS a farm cat. She was a little tabby, with fine big whiskers and a nice long tail.

Punch was the farm dog. He was a big collie with a bushy tail and a very loud bark. He didn't like cats one little bit and Tibs didn't like dogs.

Tibs hardly ever went near Punch unless he was tied up, because she knew he would chase her, and Punch was always on the watch for her so that he could tear after her and send her flying up to the top of the wall hissing and spitting. Then he would bark the place down!

Now, one day when Punch was tied up he came out

into the yard on his long chain to sniff at a garden roller that somebody had left there. He walked round it – and somehow or other his chain got twisted, and he couldn't get back to his kennel. There he was, held tightly by the garden roller, his chain pulling at his neck.

Punch pulled at it. He rolled over to try to get it loose – and all that happened was that he twisted his chain so much that it almost choked him!

He couldn't bark; he could only make a whine or a growl. So nobody heard him and nobody came to help him. He choked and struggled, but his chain was too tightly twisted round the heavy garden roller for him to get free.

Only Tibs, the farm cat, heard the noises he was making. She jumped on to the top of the wall and looked at poor Punch. What peculiar noises! What was the matter with him?

'Tibs!' croaked Punch. 'Help me. I'm choking.'

Tibs jumped down and had a look. No, she couldn't

help him. She didn't know anything about chains! But she was sorry for Punch, and she thought of something else. She ran to the farmhouse and mewed loudly.

Mrs Straws, the farmer's wife, came to the door. 'What is it?' she said. Tibs ran a little way away and looked back. The farmer's wife followed her – and then she too heard the strange noises that Punch was making out in the yard.

She went to see what they were – and in a minute or two she had undone the chain, untwisted it, patted poor Punch and given him a long drink of water!

Punch looked at Tibs on the wall. 'Thank you,' he said. 'You can come down and sit near me. I shall never chase you again. You saved me from choking.'

But Tibs didn't really trust him. She would never come down from the wall. Still, they had many a talk together and that was nice for both of them.

Then one day Tibs didn't come. She didn't come for three days, and then she told Punch why.

'I've got four little kittens,' she told him proudly.

'They're my very own. They're in the kitchen. But I do wish the children would leave them alone. They are always pulling them about, and it worries me.'

The next day Tibs looked even more worried. 'Bobby took one of my kittens and dropped it,' she said. 'I'm going to take them away from the kitchen. I shall put them in the barn.'

So she took each of her kittens by the neck and carried them one by one to a corner of the barn. But the children found them there and took them back to the kitchen again. They were like live toys to them, and they wanted to play with them!

Tibs was unhappy. She liked the children and she didn't want to scratch them. 'But what am I to do, Punch?' she said. 'One of my kittens has a bad leg because Bobby squeezed it too hard yesterday. I wish I could think of somewhere else to take them.'

Punch listened, his big head on one side. 'I know a place where nobody would ever find them,' he said. 'But I don't think you'd like it. It's a place where nobody would ever, ever look.'

'Where?' asked Tibs.

'Here in my kennel!' said Punch. 'There's plenty of good warm straw – and plenty of room for you and your kittens at the back. I promise not to sit on you. I'll be very, very careful. You were good to me once – now let me be kind to you!'

Tibs thought about it. Did she trust Punch or didn't she? He was a dog. She was a cat. She didn't know if they could really be friends. Still – she would try!

So, when nobody was about, Tibs carried each of her kittens by its neck all the way from the kitchen to the yard where the kennel was. One by one she laid the little things in the warm straw at the back. Then she settled down on them herself, purring happily.

Punch was very good. He didn't even let his tail rest on the kittens, and he gave them all the room he could. He even licked them when Tibs wasn't there, and when one of them patted his nose he was surprised and delighted.

The children looked all over the place for the kittens. They called and called Tibs. But she didn't come. She wasn't going to give her hiding place away! Her kittens were safe and happy now. Punch sat in his kennel, so that nobody could even peep in. Aha! Look where you like, Bobby and Betty, you won't find the kittens!

'It's nice to have a friend,' purred Tibs. 'Nobody knows where I am. Keep my secret, Punch.'

He will, of course – and we certainly won't tell Bobby and Betty, will we?

The Poor Little Owl

The Poor Little Owl

IN THE field nearby lived a little brown owl. John and Betty often saw it sitting on the telegraph wires in the dusk when they went to bed.

'Tvit, tvit, tvit!' said the little owl to them, and the children called 'Tvit, tvit!' back to it. It wasn't very big, and when it spread its wings it flew very silently indeed.

Then one evening, as John and Betty walked home, they saw the little owl disappear into a hole in an old, old willow tree.

'I guess it has got its nest there!' said John in excitement. 'I wonder if there will be any baby owls.

We must watch and see.'

But before they could, a sad thing happened to the little owl. It went to drink from the pond one night, overbalanced, fell into the water and couldn't get out! So in the morning John and Betty found that it was drowned, and they were very sad.

'Oh, John – what about the baby owls, if there are any in the tree?' said Betty in tears. 'There won't be anyone to feed them. They will starve to death, poor things.'

John spoke to the gardener about the owl's nest, which he was sure was in the old willow tree. 'Couldn't you look and see if there are any baby owls there?' he said. 'We don't want them to starve, you know.'

'I'm not going after any owls,' said the gardener at once. 'Dangerous creatures they are, with their sharp claws! My goodness, even a baby owl can get its claws into you so hard that you can't get them out.'

'Oh,' said John. He went away, but he kept on and

on thinking about the owls. He felt sure they were hungry and unhappy.

'Betty, there must be some way of getting them out,' he said. 'Do think. You're clever at thinking.'

So Betty thought. 'Well,' she said, 'if their claws are so sharp and strong that they can dig right into your hand and not let it go, what about letting down something into the nest – a handkerchief, perhaps – and letting them dig their claws into that? Then all we need to do is to draw up the handkerchief and the owls will come too!'

'Marvellous idea!' cried John. And so it was. Betty borrowed a big old silk hanky from Father's drawer, and the two children went to the old willow tree. They climbed up it and came to the hole, which went deep into a thick branch of the tree.

A faint hissing noise came up from the hole. 'Goodness, is there a snake in there?' asked Betty.

'No! Owls do hiss, you know,' said John. 'Now, Betty, where's the hanky? Hand it over.'

John took the hanky and let one end slowly down into the hole. There were two baby owls in the tree. They turned themselves over so that their clawed feet were on top – and how they attacked that silk hanky! They dug their feet into it and their claws caught in the silk.

'Got them – it worked!' shouted John, and he pulled up the hanky. There were the two fluffy baby owls holding on to it for all they were worth! John popped them into a box he had brought with him, shut the lid, and then switched his torch on to see the nest.

'There isn't really any nest,' he called to Betty, 'just a few shavings from the hole, that's all. But wait a minute – what's this?'

The light of his torch had shone on to something red. John put his hand into the hole and felt what it was. It seemed to be a little bag of some sort. He pulled at it – and it came out. It was heavy.

'Betty! The owl had made her nest on top of this

little bag!' cried John. 'Look, it's got the name of the bank on it. I do believe it's the diamonds that a thief stole from the bank last winter! He must have hidden it here and then forgotten where the hiding place was!'

'Goodness!' said Betty as John opened the little red bag and a whole heap of shining diamonds winked up at them. 'What a lot of diamonds! Come and tell Mummy.'

Well, that was a most exciting afternoon. The children had two baby owls to look after, and a bag of diamonds to give back to the bank! And what do you think? The bank manager gave the children a reward!

'That's for you,' he said. 'Buy what you like with it.'

So what do you think they bought with the money? They went to the shops and bought a marvellous cage in which to keep their two baby owls! It was strong wire mesh outside, and had wooden perches inside, and was very grand and big indeed.

'You can keep your little owls there and bring them up in safety till they are big enough to fly away and look after themselves,' said their mother. 'You must feed them well, give them fresh water, and clean out their cage every single day.'

So they did, and soon the two owls grew used to Betty and John and would sit quietly on their perches while the children were feeding them and cleaning out their cage. Betty and John were very proud of them, because no one else at school had owls, and even the teacher came to see them, and said what strange and curious birds they were.

'They look rather like little feathered cats!' she said. And so they did as they sat side by side on their perches, their big golden eyes looking solemnly at the visitor.

And now they have flown away to look after themselves, but John and Betty have left the cage door open in case they might like to come back there to sleep. I expect they will sometimes.

Every night the two little birds call to their friends and say 'Tvit, tvit, tvit!' from the nearby field. I wonder if you have heard them. They call so sharply and so loudly that I shouldn't be a bit surprised if you heard them too!

Hurrah for the Pepperpot!

Hurrah for the Pepperpot!

TWO FAMILIES of mice lived in the old kitchen. One was Mrs Whisker Mouse's family and the other was Mrs Furry Mouse's.

They sometimes used to visit one another when the kitchen cat was not about. When Mrs Whisker's youngest mouse, Paddy-Paws, had a party, all Mrs Furry's children were most excited.

You should have seen the way that Mrs Furry dressed them up! The boys had red trousers and blue coats, the girls had tiny blue skirts and little shawls. They really looked most amusing.

They set off to the party. Mrs Furry first of all put

her nose out of her hole to make quite sure the cat wasn't in the kitchen. She sniffed. She could smell no cat. But she could smell cheese up on the table! A meal was laid there for the farmer. Mrs Furry made up her mind that she would have a look at that cheese when the party was over. She set off across the kitchen with her little family.

The party was great fun. There were cheese cakes, bacon rind sandwiches and potato peel pies. After the meal they all played games, and they squeaked and squealed so loudly that they didn't hear the big kitchen cat come stealing into the kitchen.

But he heard their squeaks and squeals! He blinked his big green eyes and sat himself down in a dark corner to wait until the mouse family came by.

When the party was over, Mrs Furry and her family came quietly out of Mrs Whisker's hole. 'We'll just go up on to the table and see if we can nibble a bit of cheese!' whispered Mrs Furry to her four children. 'Come along! We can climb up the tablecloth. It nearly touches the ground at the corners of the table.'

So they all ran to the tablecloth and were up it in an instant! The cat was cross. It had hoped they were going straight to their hole. Then it could have caught them.

Now, as the mice were climbing up to the table, Mrs Furry caught a smell of cat. She was frightened at once. Oh dear, where could the cat be? She stood on the table and sniffed and sniffed.

'That cat is somewhere about!' she whispered to her four children. 'Keep up here with me. Don't move! Oh, if only I knew whether the cat is over there – or by the sink – or sitting just by our own hole! It is so dark that I can't see a thing.' The five mice sat as still as could be. So did the cat. They were all listening for each other. But nobody made a sound. Not one single sound.

So the cat didn't know where the mice were and the mice didn't know where the cat was.

'Mother, surely we haven't got to stay here all

night!' whispered one of the little mice. 'Why, when daylight comes we shall be easily seen.'

'Oh dear, if only I knew where that cat is!' said Mrs Furry. 'How could I find out?'

She ran a few steps over the tablecloth and bumped into something hard. It was the pepperpot. And then Mrs Furry had a really splendid idea! She went back to her little family.

'Get out your hankies and bury your noses in them,' she whispered. 'I'm going to shake the pepperpot as hard as I can, all round the edge of the table. Then, if the cat is anywhere near, he will sneeze loudly when the pepper gets up his nose. But you mustn't sneeze and give away where we are – so get out your hankies!'

Then all the little mice got out their hankies and put their sharp little noses into them. Mrs Furry picked up the pepperpot and ran to the edge of the table with it.

Shake-shake-shake! She emptied a whole lot of pepper on to the floor. Then she went to the other side.

Shake-shake-shake! Down went some more yellow pepper, flying through the air. Shake-shake-shake! Shake-shake-shake!

And then a most tremendous sneeze came up from the floor! The cat had got some pepper up his nose and he simply could not stop himself from sneezing!

'A-TISHOO!' he went. 'A-TISHOO!'

Mrs Furry scampered back to her family. 'The cat is over by the sink!' she whispered. 'Come along, slip down this side of the table, and run for your hole!'

Down they all went and scampered across the kitchen as fast as they could go. The cat heard them, but another enormous sneeze came and nearly took his head off.

'A-TISHOO!' he went, just as the last mouse squeezed down the hole.

'Hurrah for the pepperpot!' cried Mrs Furry.

And 'Hurrah, hurrah!' cried all the little mice.

Adventure in the Woods

Adventure in the Woods

ONE BEAUTIFUL moonlit night Johnny couldn't sleep. He sat up in bed and saw the moonlight streaming over his bed. Shadow, his lovely sheepdog, was lying at the foot on an old rug.

When Johnny sat up, Shadow awoke. He lifted his big head, cocked his ears and looked at his master.

'Shadow! I can't sleep!' said Johnny. 'It's too beautiful a night to waste. Let's go for a walk on the hills, shall we? Just you and I together?'

'Woof!' said Shadow in a low voice, for he knew they must not wake Johnny's father and mother. The boy slid out of bed and dressed quickly. Then he and Shadow crept out of the room and were soon in the farmyard.

The moonlight shone down and everything could be clearly seen. The ducks were on the pond, quacking, and Jessie, the farmyard dog, lay outside her kennel awake.

'Where are you going?' she asked Shadow in surprise.

'Out for a walk with Johnny!' said Shadow joyously, wagging his plumy tail. 'I've never done this before – gone out in the moonlight. I've often wondered why people don't do it – the world is lovely and pale and quiet then. We're going out on the hills.'

They were soon there. The sheep lay dotted on the hillside half asleep. Rafe and Tinker greeted Shadow as he and Johnny passed them.

'Hallo! You're out late, aren't you?'

'Off for a walk with Johnny,' said Shadow proudly. 'Where are Bob and Dandy, the other dogs?'

'Bob's over there, outside the shepherd's hut,' said

Tinker. 'I don't know where Dandy is. He went off early this morning and hasn't come back. You know what he is for wandering away. Still, we're pretty busy with the sheep just now – I'm surprised he hasn't turned up.'

The big sheepdog wagged his tail at Shadow and then lay down quietly again. Johnny patted Tinker and Rafe and went up the hill, Shadow close beside him.

Shadow wondered where Dandy had got to. It was strange that he hadn't returned before night. He ran beside Johnny, sniffing at all the smells they passed, enjoying the moonlight walk.

Then suddenly he heard a faint and faraway sound. It was so distant that at first Shadow didn't think he had heard anything. Then it came again. The big sheepdog stood still, his ears cocked well up.

'Come on, old boy,' said Johnny. 'What are you standing there like that for? There's no one about tonight. Come on, I want to get over the hill.'

Shadow trotted on again. Then, on the wind, there came that faint sound once more. Shadow stood still and listened, puzzled.

'Shadow! Whatever's the matter with you?' shouted back Johnny impatiently. 'I shan't take you out at night again if you don't keep up with me.'

Shadow ran to his little master once more, but his ears were listening all the time. And when the wind blew around him again, bringing with it that faint sound, Shadow knew what it was.

It was the faraway whine of a dog in pain. And that dog must be Dandy!

Shadow looked at Johnny. The boy was running down the other side of the hill. The moon was so bright that Shadow could even see the pattern on his sweater. Johnny was all right. He knew his way back. Shadow felt that he really must go and see what had happened to Dandy.

He stood and barked loudly to Johnny, hoping that the boy would understand. Then he turned and ran quickly down the hill again, into the valley, and made for the woods that lay on the next hill to the east.

Johnny was puzzled when Shadow disappeared. He called and whistled, but Shadow was out of hearing. The boy went back a little way to see if the sheepdog was rabbiting, but there was no sign of him.

It's too bad of Shadow, thought Johnny vexed. *He always keeps up with me when he is out for a walk. Why should he leave me? I won't take him out again!*

He went on by himself, wondering where Shadow was. The sheepdog was far away by that time, running tirelessly on his strong legs. He came to the wood, and then the wailing sound he had heard came again, much louder because it was nearer.

It is *Dandy!* thought Shadow. *Poor old Dandy. What can have happened?*

He ran swiftly towards the sound and came to where Dandy was lying in the wood. Shadow ran up to him and barked. 'What's up? Why don't you come home?'

Dandy answered with a pitiful whine. Then Shadow saw that the poor dog had his foot caught in a steel trap. It had been set for rabbits, and was a cruel thing with steel teeth that bit into an animal's leg and held it fast. Dandy hadn't seen it and had put his foot right into it. Now he was held tight and was in great pain. The trap was too heavy for him to move or he might have dragged it along with him.

Shadow tore at it with his teeth, but Dandy stopped him. 'That's no use,' he said. 'I know these traps. I can only get my foot out if someone opens the trap, and only people know how to do that. You can't open it.'

'I'll go and fetch someone who can,' said Shadow, and he looked anxiously at Dandy, who had lain his head down wearily on his good paw. The dog was tired out with pain.

Shadow ran off, his heart beating fast because he ran so swiftly. He must get help for Dandy. He must not let him suffer one minute more pain than he could help. How his poor foot must hurt him! How wicked those steel traps were!

Shadow ran back to the farm. Johnny had got back now and was in his bedroom, about to take off his sweater. Shadow padded into the room and went up to him. But Johnny pushed him away.

'Shadow, I don't want you! You left me tonight. The moon might have gone in and left me in the dark, and I might have got lost. I am ashamed of you. Go away.'

Shadow's heart sank when he heard Johnny talk to him like that. He licked his hand, but the boy took it away. Then Shadow took hold of his sleeve and gave it a gentle tug. That meant, 'Please come with me!'

'If you think I'm going to take you out for a walk again, you're wrong,' said Johnny crossly. 'And I don't want you to sleep on my bed tonight. If you're going to run off and leave me when I want you, I don't want you to sleep with me.'

Shadow felt as if his heart was breaking. Johnny had never said such a thing to him before. The dog pressed himself close to the boy and licked wherever he could. His tail drooped down. Then he took the corner of Johnny's sweater in his mouth and tugged it again.

Johnny looked down into the soft brown eyes. Shadow was speaking to him as clearly as could be. 'Come with me,' his eyes were saying.

Johnny was puzzled. 'Well, I'll come,' he said at last. 'But if it's just for nothing, I shall be cross with you.'

Shadow took Johnny into the moonlit farmyard once more, and then took the path to the woods. Johnny followed, more and more puzzled. But when at last he stood looking down at Dandy he knew why Shadow had run from him, and why the dog had tugged at his sweater!

'Oh, Dandy! What's wrong?' cried Johnny, and he knelt down beside the tired dog. The moonlight glinted on the bright trap, and Johnny gave a cry of dismay.

'You've got your foot in a trap! Oh, Dandy, you poor poor thing! How long have you been here? Oh, how am I to open the trap?'

Dandy whined a little. He was so tired out with pain that he could hardly lift his head. Shadow pulled at the trap. Johnny looked at it carefully and saw how to open it. He must put his foot on one part, and then drag open the steel teeth.

The boy tried – and at last the cruel teeth parted, and there was Dandy's foot, free, but crushed and bleeding. The dog did not know at first that his foot was free, for it still hurt him terribly.

'Take your foot out before the trap shuts again!' cried Johnny. And Dandy painfully moved his poor foot. He stood up on three legs, holding his wounded foot high. It still hurt, though with a different pain now. But at any rate he was free. He could get away from that horrible steel thing that had held him prisoner!

The three of them went home slowly, for Dandy was tired.

Johnny woke his father and the two of them gently bathed and bound up the hurt foot.

'Dandy, if you *will* go off hunting by yourself like this, you *must* learn to look out for traps!' said the farmer. 'Poor creature, you won't be much use looking after the sheep for a week or two. But your foot will mend. Go and sleep in the yard with Jessie the farm dog tonight.'

Dandy trotted off on three legs. He licked Shadow as he went.

'Thank you,' he said. 'You're a good friend. No wonder Johnny loves you best in the world!'

But that's just what he doesn't do! thought Shadow sadly as he lay down by the kitchen fire. *Johnny has said tonight that he doesn't want me on his bed. He is angry because I left him. But how could I leave Dandy in pain?*

Johnny wondered where Shadow was. He was now in bed, waiting for the sheepdog to come and jump up on his feet. But Shadow didn't come.

Surely he doesn't think I'm still cross with him! thought Johnny.

He went to the kitchen – and there was Shadow by the fire, ears and tail well down. 'Shadow!' cried Johnny. 'Come here! I want you on my bed. I think you're a good clever dog to find poor Dandy like that and fetch me to him. I understand why you left me now – and you were quite right. I'm sorry I was cross. Come here, Shadow!'

And Shadow came gladly, whining a little and licking the boy's bare legs. He lay down happily on Johnny's bed, nibbling the boy's toes with love. Nothing in the world mattered so long as Johnny wanted him close!

Black Bibs

Black Bibs

ONCE UPON a time, at the beginning of the New Year, the little brown house sparrows noticed that the starlings were growing beautiful green, violet and purple colours in their feathers. They saw that the little chaffinch had put on a much brighter pink waistcoat, and that the blackbird seemed to have dipped his beak in gold.

'Why?' they said to the starlings. 'Why?' to the chaffinch, and, 'Why?' to the blackbird.

'Because spring is coming!' they all answered. 'We shall soon be looking for our little wives – and we like to be dressed in our best then! Why don't *you* do something about it, sparrows? Cock and hen sparrows are exactly the same in the way they dress! You might at least try to dress a little differently in springtime, so that when you go wooing your mates they may think you look handsome!'

'That is a good idea,' said the cock sparrows. 'We will go to Dabble the elf and ask her if she'll use her dyes to colour our feathers a bit!'

So they flew off to Dabble. She was indoors and the house was shut. The sparrows hopped up the path, and were just going to ring the bell when one said, 'We haven't yet decided what colour to ask for.'

'We'll have red vests,' said a big cock sparrow.

'Silly idea!' said another. 'We don't want to look like those stuck-up robins.'

'Well, let's have yellow tails and green beaks,' said another.

'And be laughed at by everyone!' screamed a fourth sparrow. 'No, we'll have blue wings and blue chests – very smart indeed.'

'I want pink legs, I want pink legs,' chirruped another.

'Be quiet and don't be silly,' said the one next to him. 'Do you want to look as if you're walking on primrose stalks? They're pink too.'

'Chirrup, chirrup, chirrup!' shouted all the excited sparrows at once, and each began to yell out what he wanted – red head, yellow beak, green chest, pink wings, white tail and the rest. Really, you never in your life heard such a deafening noise!

Dabble the elf was having a snooze on her bed. She woke up in a hurry and wondered what the dreadful noise was. She opened her window and looked out. Her garden was full of screeching sparrows, pecking at one another and stirring up the dust.

'Be quiet!' said Dabble.

'Chirrup, chirrup, chirrup,' screamed the sparrows. Then they caught sight of Dabble and shouted at her loudly: 'We want to ask you to give us something that will make us look different from the hen sparrows –

blue legs, or pink wings – or something.'

'Oh, I'll give you something, all right!' said Dabble crossly. 'Come in, one by one.'

So the sparrows went in one by one at her front door – and were pushed out one by one at her back door – and when they came out they were wearing little black bibs under their chins! Yes, every one of them!

'*Babies!* Quarrelsome *babies*, that's all you are!' said Dabble, shutting the door on the last one. 'And babies wear bibs – so you can wear them too!'

And it's a funny thing, but since that day every cock sparrow has to wear a black bib under his chin in the springtime. You look and see!

The Foolish Frog

The Foolish Frog

THERE WAS once a frog who was really very foolish. He thought he knew everything. When he was a tadpole he swam around telling everyone what nasty leggy things frogs were – but even when he found that he was growing into a frog himself that didn't make him ashamed of his foolishness! No, he just went on being as boastful and as stupid as ever.

In the autumn, when the nights were frosty, the frogs began to think of going to sleep at the bottom of the pond, head downwards in the oozy mud. The toads hopped slowly out of the water and went to some damp stones they knew. They crept underneath, shut their bright coppery eyes and went to sleep there. They would not wake up until the warm springtime. But the foolish frog thought it was a waste of time to sleep through so many months. He didn't want to snooze under a stone. He didn't want to sleep in the mud at the bottom of the pond. No, he wanted to be up and about like the rabbits and the mice!

'It is a stupid idea to sleep so much of your lives away!' he said to the other frogs when they told him it was time to prepare for the winter sleep. 'Why should you be afraid of the winter? What does it matter if it is cold? I shan't mind!'

'You think you are so clever!' said the other frogs scornfully. 'Very well, keep awake all the winter through if it pleases you! We shan't mind!'

So they left the foolish frog, swam down to the bed of the pond, tucked themselves into the mud and were soon sound asleep. They forgot the cold, they forgot the lack of flies and grubs – they slept peacefully and happily.

But the foolish frog still swam about in the pond. He wondered where the flies had gone that used to skim on the surface, and which tasted so good. He climbed out of the water and went to look for some in the ditch. But there were no flies, no caterpillars, no slugs to be found. The little frog felt very hungry.

He went back to the water and swam around sadly. Perhaps it would be a good idea after all to go to sleep. It wasn't much good being awake and hungry!

'Well, I'll go and have a nap in the mud,' said the foolish frog at last. 'But I shall not sleep all the winter through, as the others do. No, at the first possible moment, when the sun is warm, I shall wake up and enjoy myself again!'

He was soon asleep. He slept all through the month of December, and almost all through January. Then there came a warm spell. The sun shone on the pond and the frogs felt the warmth and stirred in their sleep. The foolish frog woke right up. Ah! How warm the water felt! Surely the winter was over!

He swam up to the surface. It was lovely in the sunshine. He swam down to the mud and woke up all the other frogs.

'Come!' he said. 'The winter is over! The sun is shining. Wake up, and come and play.'

But the oldest frog, after he had taken one look out of the water, swam back to the mud.

'Take no notice of the foolish one,' he said. 'Winter is not over. This is just a warm spell. It will be colder than ever soon. Bury your heads in the mud again, brothers and sisters, and go to sleep.'

The frogs obeyed him – all but the foolish frog, who was very angry. He swam up to the surface by himself and enjoyed the warm sunshine – but, when night came, and the sun went, something strange happened to the pond. The water became hard instead of soft, and icy cold. The pond was freezing! The water was turning into ice! The frog did not know what was happening and he was frightened. He swam around, but every minute it became more difficult.

The moon came out and shone on the freezing pond. It shone on the poor foolish frog, now held tightly in the thickening ice. The frog opened his mouth and croaked mournfully.

A wandering hedgehog heard him and was surprised. A frog croaking at this time of year! How could that be? He peered about and saw the frog in the ice. He pattered across the hard pond and breathed down on the trapped frog.

'Friend, you are in a bad way,' said the hedgehog. 'You will be dead by morning unless I can help you. If I lie down by you I may melt the ice a little. Then you must struggle hard and kick out with your legs, and maybe you will get free of the ice.'

The heat of the hedgehog's body thawed the ice a little and the frog found that he was able to move around. He kicked out strongly with his legs and managed to get free. In a second he was hopping on the icy pond, and the hedgehog hurried away to the bank beside him.

'There is an old stone here in the ditch,' said the kindly hedgehog. 'Get under that and sleep for the rest of the winter, frog. You should not be awake now.'

'Thank you,' said the frog humbly, for once really ashamed of himself, and very much frightened at his narrow escape.

He crept under the stone, shut his eyes and fell soundly asleep.

He was awakened by the croaking of the frogs in the pond. It was springtime now, and they had all awakened in excitement, glad to think the warm days had come again. They wondered where the foolish frog had gone.

'I expect he got frozen into the ice and is dead,' said the oldest frog scornfully. 'He was foolish enough for anything!'

That made the foolish frog very angry. He hopped out from under his stone and stared rudely at the old frog.

'No, I was not frozen into the ice,' he croaked untruthfully. 'I had a very much finer winter than you did!'

'Oh, there is the foolish frog after all!' croaked all the other frogs in surprise. 'Come into the pond and play, brother. Choose a nice little wife for yourself so that she may lay you eggs to grow into tadpoles!'

'I shall find a little pond where no other frogs are!' said the foolish frog. 'My wife shall lay her eggs there, and we shall know that all the tadpoles in our little pond are ours! We shall teach them not to speak to or play with your tadpoles!'

With that he hopped off. Soon he met a pretty little green frog and asked her to be his wife. Then they went to find a nice little pond where she could lay her eggs.

The foolish frog found a large puddle left by the rain. 'This will do nicely,' he said to his green wife. 'Come along!'

The little green frog laid many eggs in the puddle.

The two frogs lived there contentedly, though all the toads and frogs that passed laughed at them scornfully.

The sun shone out warmly. The puddle grew smaller as the sun dried it. It grew smaller still. The little green frog became afraid and hopped off to the big pond. But the foolish frog stayed with the jelly-like eggs, hoping that they would soon hatch.

The puddle grew very small indeed – and then, alas, it dried up altogether! The mass of frogspawn dried up too, and the foolish frog was left in a hole by the side of the lane that led to the pond.

But still he would not move. He waited for the puddle to fill again. Soon, down the lane, there came the sound of clip-clopping hooves. The old farm horse was coming. She came nearer to the hole – nearer and nearer. One of her great hooves trod on the mass of dried frogspawn and another almost squashed the frightened frog to bits. He leapt out of the way and only his left hind foot was hurt.

Full of fear he hopped away to the pond and leapt

into the cool water. His foot hurt him and he had lost his eggs – they would never hatch now. He was ashamed and miserable.

'Here is the foolish frog back again,' croaked all the others. 'Well, brother, did your eggs hatch into tadpoles in that puddle? Have you told them not to speak to our young ones?'

The foolish frog said nothing. He sank down to the mud and lay there, his foot aching.

I am indeed foolish, he thought to himself. *I thought I knew everything, but I know nothing. I will be humble in future and listen to what the others say.*

Now he is no longer proud and foolish. He does what he is told. He listens to the older frogs. He is becoming wise and humble. Soon he will no longer be known as the foolish frog.

But you will always be able to tell him by his left hind foot. It got better but it grew crooked, so if you see a frog with a foot like that you will know that he once was the foolish little frog!

The Little Lost Hen

The Little Lost Hen

ONE AFTERNOON, when Harry was coming home from school, he saw a little red hen. That doesn't sound very surprising, but when I tell you that the hen was just about to cross the road in the busy street, all by itself, you will see why Harry was rather astonished.

'Goodness!' said Harry in surprise. 'What is that hen doing in the middle of the town all by itself? It will get run over if it tries to cross this busy street. It must have escaped from somewhere and got lost.'

A car hooted at the hen and it ran back to the kerb, fluttering its red feathers and squawking loudly. Harry was worried. What was he to do? You couldn't tell a hen to go home, as you could tell a dog.

There's nothing to be done but to pick up the hen and take it home with me, thought Harry. *I can put it into my nursery until I know who the owner is.*

Now, Harry wasn't very good at picking up birds. Some people love picking up anything, and don't mind touching worms or spiders. It is good to be like that, but Harry wasn't. He shivered when he tried to pick up the hen. He didn't like it at all.

The hen was so frightened that she let herself be picked up without struggling a bit. Harry managed to get her under his left arm, and held her there with his right hand. She tried to peck him and he nearly dropped her. But he just managed to hold on, and off he went home, with the hen under his arm.

When he got home he called for his mother, but she was out. Jane, the maid, was in the garden hanging out some tea cloths. So Harry went into the house by himself, carrying the little lost hen.

He went to his room and looked around. Where

could he put the hen to make her comfortable? He saw his barrow there, and he carefully put the hen into it.

But she was out at once and ran clucking all around the room because she didn't know where she was.

'Oh, hen, don't be so silly,' said Harry. 'Are you hungry? Stop pecking at my soldiers, please!'

Harry went out and shut the door. He went to the cupboard where Mother kept the seed for her pigeons and got a handful from a bag. Then back he went to his room.

'Kuk-kuk-kuk-kuk-kuk!' said the hen, running to Harry.

'Kuk-kuk,' answered the boy, and threw a handful of seed on the carpet. The hen pecked it up greedily. Then she cocked her bright-eyed head on one side and looked at Harry.

'Kuk-kuk-kuk!' she said in a very kindly tone.

Harry didn't understand what she said, but what she meant was that she thought he was a very kind little boy. She began to peck up the rest of the seed.

Then Harry heard his mother's voice and he flew downstairs to tell her about the little lost hen. But Mother had a visitor with her, and Harry had to be quiet and not say a word except how do you do. Mother wouldn't let him talk when visitors were there, unless he was spoken to.

But after a while Mother heard a peculiar noise from Harry's room, and she frowned.

'I wonder what that funny noise upstairs is,' she said. 'It's very odd!'

Everybody listened – and they could hear the hen clucking loudly. Then suddenly she cackled at the top of her voice!

'Cackle-cackle-cackle, cluck, cluck, cluck!'

'It sounds like a hen!' said Mother in astonishment. 'Well, I never!'

'It is a hen!' said Harry, and he told his mother all about the little hen he had found trying to cross the street.

'Harry! Do you really mean to say that you put the

hen in your room?' said Mother. 'Oh, whatever will you do next?'

'It must be Mrs White's hen,' said the visitor, Miss Brown. 'She told me this morning that her favourite red hen had escaped, and she didn't know where it had gone!'

'Oh, then, do you mind taking it back to her?' cried Harry. 'The poor little hen feels so strange in my room. It would be so pleased to go back home again to all its friends.'

'Of course I will,' said Miss Brown, and they all went upstairs. There was the hen, scratching at the carpet, and clucking softly to itself. It ran to Harry and pecked at a freckle on his legs. Miss Brown picked it up.

'Would you like a basket to take it home in?' asked Harry's mother.

'Oh, no. I like the nice soft warm feeling of a hen,' said Miss Brown, cuddling the little red hen to her. 'My word, won't Mrs White be pleased when she sees me walking in with her lost hen? It is her very favourite one, and lays her a big brown egg every day.'

'I love brown eggs,' said Harry. 'They taste much nicer than white ones. I wish I had a hen that laid me brown eggs.'

'We haven't room in our garden to keep hens,' said Mother. 'Well, goodbye, Miss Brown, and I do hope the hen will behave itself and not try to get out of your arms!'

Miss Brown and the hen went away. Harry felt quite lonely without the little red hen in his room. He wandered around by himself, wondering what to play with. He thought he would play with the soldiers in his toy fort.

So he went over to the fort – but before he could pick up any of his soldiers he saw something that made him stare and stare!

In the very middle of his toy fort was a big brown egg! Yes, there it lay among the soldiers, big and brown and smooth. Harry gave a scream of joy and picked it up. It was warm – as warm as toast!

'Mother! Mother! Come and look here!' yelled Harry. 'Oh, quick, do come!'

Mother came rushing in – and when she saw the egg she laughed and laughed.

'Well, really, Harry, this is the funniest thing I ever heard of! You find a hen and bring it to your room and feed it – and it lays an egg in your toy fort! I will ring up Mrs White and tell her, and you can take the egg round to her in a basket.'

So Mother rang up Mrs White and told her. When she put down the telephone she turned to Harry.

'Mrs White says that the hen must have meant the egg for *you*, Harry, in return for your kindness,' said Mother. 'She says you are to keep it and eat it for breakfast!'

'Oh, Mother! What a surprise! And I do so like brown eggs!' said Harry in delight. 'How kind of the hen to think of me like that!'

So Harry had the brown egg for his breakfast, and

he told me that it was the very nicest one he had ever had in his life. Wasn't he lucky?

The Goldfish That Grew

The Goldfish That Grew

HOPPETTY HAD a goldfish in a glass bowl, the prettiest little thing you could wish to see, and the pixie was very proud of it indeed. But what puzzled him was that it didn't grow! It kept as small as could be, and Hoppetty became quite worried about it.

'I give it plenty of good food,' he said, 'and it has a nice piece of green waterweed in the bowl, and a little black water snail for company. I do wonder why it doesn't grow.'

But nobody could tell him why.

'Perhaps it isn't very happy,' said Mrs Biscuit, the baker's wife. 'I've heard it said that unhappy creatures never grow much.'

Hoppetty couldn't bear to think that.

I'm very kind to it, he thought. *It ought to be happy. How dreadful if people should think it doesn't grow because I'm unkind to it and make it unhappy!*

He gave the fish more food than ever, but it wouldn't eat it. The water snail feasted on it instead, and that made Hoppetty cross. He really didn't know what to do!

Then one day, as he walked over Bumblebee Common, he saw a pointed hat sticking up among the gorse bushes, and he knew a witch was somewhere nearby. Hoppetty peeped to see.

Yes, sure enough, a witch was there, sitting on the ground beside a little fire she had made. On it she had placed a kettle, which was boiling merrily. Soon she took it off and held over the flames a little fish she had caught in the river nearby. She meant to have it for her dinner.

The fish was very small and the witch was hungry.

'I could eat a much bigger fish than you!' Hoppetty heard her say to the little dead trout. 'I think I'll make you bigger, and then I shall have a fine meal!'

She laid the fish down on the grass, and waved her hand over it twice. 'Little fish, bigger grow, I shall like you better so!' she chanted, and then said a very magic word that made Hoppetty shiver and shake, it was so full of enchantment. But goodness! How he stared to see what happened next! The little fish began to grow, and grow, and presently the witch took it up and held it once more over the flames, smiling to see what a fine meal she had!

A great idea came to Hoppetty. He would run straight home, and say the spell over his little goldfish! Then it really would grow, and everyone would be so surprised.

Off went Hoppetty, never stopping to think that it was wrong to peep and pry and use someone else's spell when they did not know he had heard it. He didn't stop running until he got home, and then he went straight to his little goldfish swimming about in its bowl.

He waved his hand over it twice. 'Little fish, bigger grow, I shall like you better so!' he chanted, and then he said the very magic word, though it made him shiver and shake to do so.

All at once the goldfish gave a little leap in the water, and began to grow! How it grew! Hoppetty couldn't believe his eyes! It was soon twice as big as before, and still it went on growing!

'You're big enough now, little fish,' said Hoppetty. 'You can stop growing.'

But the fish didn't! It went on and on getting bigger and bigger, and soon it was too big for the bowl.

'Oh dear!' said Hoppetty in dismay. 'This is very awkward. I'd better fetch my washing-up bowl and put you in that.'

He popped the fish in his washing-up bowl, but still it went on growing, and Hoppetty had to put it into his bath.

'Please, please stop!' he begged the fish. 'You're far too big, really!'

But the fish went on growing, and soon it was even too big for the bath. Then Hoppetty really didn't know what to do.

'I'd better take my fish under my arm and go and find that old witch!' he said at last. 'She can tell me how to stop my goldfish from getting any bigger. Oh dear, I do hope she won't be cross!'

He picked the goldfish up, and wrapped a wet handkerchief round its head so that it wouldn't die, and set off to Bumblebee Common. How heavy the fish was! And it kept getting heavier and heavier too, because it went on growing. Hoppetty staggered along the road with it, and everyone stared at him in surprise. Then a gnome policeman tapped him on the arm.

'You are being cruel to that fish,' he said. 'He is panting for breath, poor thing. Put him in that pond over there at once.'

Sure enough, the wet handkerchief had slipped off

the fish's head, and it was opening and shutting its mouth in despair. It wriggled and struggled, and Hoppetty could hardly hold it. He went to the pond and popped it in. It slid into the water, flicked its great tail and sent a wave right over Hoppetty's feet.

Then who should come by but that witch! Hoppetty ran to her and told her all that had happened, begging her to forgive him for using her spell.

'Do you mean to say that you were peeping and prying on me?' said the witch in a rage. 'Well, it just serves you right, you nasty little pixie! Your fish can go on growing till it's bigger than the town itself, and that will be a fine punishment for you!'

'Madam, tell the spell that will make the fish go back to its right size,' said the policeman sternly. 'Hoppetty has done wrong, but you cannot refuse his request now that he has asked your pardon.'

The witch had to obey. She went to the pond and waved her hand over it twice. 'Big fish, smaller grow, I shall like you better so!' she chanted, and then she said another magic word. At once the great goldfish shrank smaller and smaller, and at last it was its own size again. Hoppetty cried out in delight, and ran to get a net to catch it.

But that little fish wouldn't be caught! It wasn't going to go back into a tiny glass bowl again now that it had a whole pond to swim about in, and frogs and sticklebacks, snails and beetles to talk to. Oh, no!

Hoppetty had to give it up and he went sadly back home.

'I've lost my little fish,' he said, 'but it serves me right for peeping and prying. I shan't do that again!'

And I don't believe he ever did!

Acknowledgements

All efforts have been made to seek necessary permissions.

The stories in this publication first appeared in the following publications:

'The Kitten That Disappeared' first appeared in *Sunny Stories*, No. 67, 1938.

'The Tale of the Goldfish' first appeared in *Sunny Stories for Little Folks*, No. 214, 1935.

'Good Dog, Tinker!' first appeared in *Sunny Stories*, No. 315, 1943.

'Clever Old Budgie' first appeared as 'Clever Old Budgie!' in *Enid Blyton's Magazine*, No. 14, Vol. 3, 1955.

'The Cow That Lost Her Moo' first appeared in *Sunny Stories for Little Folks*, No. 237, 1936.

'A Little Bit of Magic' first appeared in *Sunny Stories*, No. 84, 1938.

'The Noah's Ark Lion' first appeared in *Sunny Stories*, No. 60, 1938.

'Silly Simon and the Goat' first appeared as 'Simple Simon and the Goat' in *Sunny Stories*, No. 326, 1944.

'The Very Little Hen' first appeared in *Sunny Stories for Little Folks*, No. 130, 1931.

'Spiny's Good Turn' first appeared in *Sunny Stories*, No. 542, 1952.

'What a Surprise!' first appeared in *Sunny Stories for Little Folks*, No. 237, 1936.

'The Old Toad and the Spider' first appeared in *Sunny Stories*, No. 147, 1939.

'Binkle's Tail' first appeared as Chapter 20 in *The Teacher's Treasury*, Vol. 1, 1926.

'The Great Big Bumblebee' first appeared as 'The Great Big Bumble-Bee' in *Sunny Stories for Little Folks*, No. 121, 1931.

'The Cat Without Whiskers' first appeared in *Sunny Stories*, No. 116, 1939.

'When the Donkey Sneezed' first appeared in *Sunny Stories for Little Folks*, No. 151, 1932.

ACKNOWLEDGEMENTS

'The Banana Robber' first appeared in *Sunny Stories for Little Folks*, No. 243, 1936.

'The Beautiful Big Bone' first appeared in *Daily Mail Annual for Boys and Girls*, 1944.

'Good Old Shelly-Back!' first appeared as 'Good Old Shelly-Back' in *Sunny Stories*, No. 239, 1936.

'Hoo-Hoo's Party' first appeared in *Sunny Stories for Little Folks*, No. 101, 1930.

'Tinker-Dog and Prince' first appeared as 'Tinker-dog and Prince' in *Sunny Stories*, No. 19, 1937.

'Boo! Boo! Boo!' first appeared as 'He Couldn't Say Boo to a Goose!' in *Sunny Stories*, No. 434, 1948.

'It's Nice to Have a Friend' first appeared in *Sunny Stories*, No. 459, 1949.

'The Poor Little Owl' first appeared in *Sunny Stories*, No. 213, 1941.

'Hurrah for the Pepperpot!' first appeared as 'Hurrah for the Pepper-Pot!' in *Sunny Stories*, No. 233, 1941.

'Adventure in the Woods' first appeared as 'An Adventure in the Woods' in *Sunny Stories*, No. 291, 1942.

'Black Bibs' first appeared in *Teachers World*, No. 1756, 1937.

'The Foolish Frog' first appeared in *Sunny Stories*, No. 164, 1940.

'The Little Lost Hen' first appeared in *Sunny Stories*, No. 228, 1941.

'The Goldfish That Grew' first appeared in *Sunny Stories for Little Folks*, No. 126, 1931.

Enid Blyton®

is one of the most popular children's authors of all time. Her books have sold over 500 million copies and have been translated into other languages more often than any other children's author.

Enid Blyton adored writing for children. She wrote over 600 books and hundreds of short stories. *The Famous Five* books, now 75 years old, are her most popular. She is also the author of other favourites including *The Secret Seven*, *The Magic Faraway Tree*, *Malory Towers* and *Noddy*.

Born in London in 1897, Enid lived much of her life in Buckinghamshire and adored dogs, gardening and the countryside. She was very knowledgeable about trees, flowers, birds and animals. Dorset – where some of the Famous Five's adventures are set – was a favourite place of hers too.

Enid Blyton's stories are read and loved by millions of children (and grown-ups) all over the world. Visit enidblyton.co.uk to discover more.